The Promise Between US

Story - Clive Dev

Chief Editor-Ashamole Clive

This is a work of fiction. Names, characters, businesses, places, events, locales and incidents are either the products of the author's imagination or used in a fictitious manner. Any resemblance to actual persons, living or dead, or actual events is purely coincidental.

OTHER BOOKS by Clive Dev

- **TRUE COLORS - The Accidental Heist**
- **STRANGERS INSIDE - Detective Dev Crime Thriller Series**
- **SOME GOOD HEARTS STILL ....-Romance (short story kindle edition)**

COMING SOON

- **THREADS OF LIFE-The turbulence**

The city of London is waking up and becoming lively in the morning. It is cold, dark and windy. The clouds have painted a black curtain over the sky which is preventing the sun from doing its job.

The people are using either public or private transport to travel to work. Some people are clad in their winter gear and braving the elements. They have decided to walk to work which is a good way of getting fresh air and physical activity. The colorful umbrellas are collapsing in the strong wind. The people using these are frustrated and are dumping them into the bins lined on the side of the street.

The roads are crowded and heavy with traffic. Some drivers are very impatient and beeping their horns. The buses are unexpectedly crowded from the weather. Regular commuters are finding it difficult to get into the bus. Those who were successful in getting on board, did not have a place to sit either. And the seats were wet with water dripping from the outer wears.

Maria found a window seat on the bus with some difficulty. She looked very professional but, also very attractive. She had a slim build, five eleven in height and dark curly hair. Her lips were full and carried a pout. It has only been a week since she arrived in London. She was transferred from the ECC bank's branch in Rome. This is her first time to work here. She is eagerly looking outside the window. Visibility is not great, but this will do for the moment. She had got some time to sightsee in the last week. But this is a good way to get to know the city. She began to look outside as soon as she had settled in her seat. The bus stopped at the next junction. A familiar figure got on the bus. Maria saw her and waved at her. She waved back and after paying the fair, she then approached the seat where Maria was sitting and sat down beside her. Maria spoke excitedly, "Hello Jennifer, I always thought that you commuted by car?" Jennifer smiled at her new friend, "Yes I do, but the weather was so bad last night, that I stayed in my apartment in the city. It is only a five-minute walk from the bus stop." Maria answered, "That's good, at least you have a solution for the bad weather." Jennifer replied, "It is a guest house for our VIP's from the suppliers to our firm. We tend to use it in case of emergencies." She sees that Maria is watching all the sights around her in excitement.

The corner shop is churning out hot donuts of various kinds-Plain, chocolate or strawberry with colorful sprinkles, mocha and vanilla flavors. Jennifer tells Maria about this shop. "I like the donuts from here. They are very tasty. It is also a story of hard work eventually paying off." She then proceeded to relate the story of a widow trying to raise her children back in the old days. She explained to her about how goods in small shop are sold in London. It is very different to what Maria has experienced in Italy. "The coffee shops around the main streets here are always busy. So are the deli's that give generous student discounts. Wraps and rolls are made according to customer request, then rolled in brown paper wraps and sealed with the price quoted stickers". They keep looking outside and passing comments about different things.

People waiting for the buses have occupied the shop fronts that have colorful awnings. It is good for the shops as it increases their business. Some of them will definitely come in and browse. Some of those may end up buying something; although it may be inconvenient for the regular shoppers to get in and out of the shop.

The clubbers are out and ready to earn some money. In spite of the pelting rain, they are warming up now. Some are strumming on their guitars for public enjoyment and some are sketch artists displaying their waterproof talents on the walkways and footpaths. Some of them are restless souls. They can do non-stop acrobatics. They are the ones at a loss because of the rain. It will not be worth the few coins, if they slip and fall.

Some can stay still for hours so they are excellent in acting as statues. These people are very skilled. The benevolent public are dropping coins of various denominations in to the hats or disposable cups that are kept nearby. The hats are being emptied by the clubbers frequently.

They do not empty the hat or the cup completely. They always leave two or three small coins inside the hat. This is to inform the public that the receptacle kept on the floor is for dropping coins and is a form of invitation to do so. This is also a trick to evoke feelings of sympathy in the passer by. This sympathy in turn, generates feelings of generosity in the subject. They also feel a compelling need to donate towards this person's cause. Anything that works!

Everyone has to make a living. Those people are not out there by choice. When the educated graduates are finding it difficult to make a living; what will be the state of the not so educated and the underprivileged? Un employment is rife in the city. And this is at least more decent. They are working hard to earn a pittance instead of begging or peddling drugs.

The tourists have vacated the hostels and are now roaming around the main street with their wheelie suitcases trailing behind them. The different tourist attractions are mainly lined in an area of eight to ten kilometers around this street. This street itself has a museum, a casino, a theatre, some hotels and some schools and colleges. There are many language schools around the main street as well.

****

The ECC bank is on the far end of the main street near Billings gate Market. They both alight from the bus at the stop directly across from the bank. It is a very large national bank of international repute. It not only caters to the residents with day to day banking facilities but, also specialises in trading of foreign currency. The bank has a large vault which has reserves of millions of Pounds and Euros at any given time. There is a large car park in the basement. There are approximately three hundred people employed by this bank.

A blue color sedan pulls up at the street parking outside the bank. The man seated in the driver seat switches off the ignition. He takes out his binoculars and looks closely at the entrance of the bank. He can see a security guard standing outside the door.

It is ten fifteen in the morning and he has already counted twenty people going into the bank in the last ten minutes. A busy bank by the looks of it! It is going to be difficult to rob this bank in the middle of the day. "Not difficult," Leo corrected himself "but there will be too many casualties". He remarked to himself, "I don't have a problem killing anyone but what is the point in taking many lives when only one or two are needed? The head count can be used for some other time."

If there are too many people in the bank at the time of the robbery, the number of people with false bravado will increase. This will lead to stupid mistakes. It is fun to challenge the police, a very special someone enters his thoughts at the moment; but it will increase the heat on them. All the banks are equipped with alarm switches which when activated, will alert the nearest police station. He could not take that risk in broad day light. The police will be here before the boys could say "Zeeboomba". They will not have enough time to even get the vault door opened. "We need a better plan-a perfect plan-challenging enough; but difficult for that someone special to solve," he decided in his head.

****

Leo then drove back to his rented house. He had been observing the bank for the past week but yet had not been able to get a fool proof plan to rob the bank. When he got home; he saw that Charlie was waiting for him on the footpath, outside his house. He looked as if he was waiting a good while. "Hiya Leo" he greeted. Leo smiled back as he parked the car on the drive and got out. He opened the door. "Come in Charlie, it is cold outside", he invited his friend into the house

Charlie walked in behind Leo and straddled a chair. Leo smiled. "Charlie always needs something between his thighs," he thought to himself. "What's up Charlie? You are visiting me very early today?" Charlie grinned sheepishly, "I am just strapped for a little bit of money." He looked at Leo and wondered loudly, "I don't know how you are able to survive after coming out of the prison, but I can barely manage. I am not finding any work." Leo regarded him with intensity, "Charlie, I don't spend all my money on drinks. You have an insatiable thirst for the booze." Charlie scratched his head and smiled, "Yeah, I know, just can't keep my hands off the intoxicating poison". Leo handed him a beer. He knew that Charlie could drink alcohol at any time of the day. He was becoming hooked. The symptoms were all there and he probably could still escape its clutches; if he tried. But there is no talking to him when it comes to alcohol.

"Where is Samuel today?" he asked? Charlie laughed, "He is holed in with a lady of the street." Leo grunted. Another one with a huge problem! He will one day, die from sexually transmitted disease if he was not careful. The ladies of the street themselves are very careful when it comes to their trade. They are professionals but you can never be too sure. Some customers don't like to use protection! The ladies sometimes agree to it reluctantly. You have no choice when money is running dry and you are strapped for cash. He smiled to himself, he was no saint either. He could do a few rounds when he felt like it. But Samuel went for the sake of the flesh and not for his own satisfaction.

While he was thinking on these lines, there was a knock on the door. Leo went to the window, moved the curtain slightly and cautiously looked out. It was Jude standing outside the door. He relaxed and opened the door. "Hello Leo, how are you? I was getting bored, so I decided to drop." Leo answered him with a smile in his eyes. "Why? Are you not watching the television today?" Jude answered him with equal gusto, "You know Leo! I like the women I can touch; than the one's I am only allowed to see?" They both laughed aloud at the sexual intonation behind Jude's words. The two men reached the living room. Jude was delighted to see Charlie. "Hola Charlie! How are you man?" Charlie smiled, "Good mate, good to see you. How are you?" They were all now sitting around the table.

Charlie was already on his second bottle of beer. Leo made tea for himself and Jude. He took out a packet of cigarettes from the cabinet beside the table and offered it to his friends. They all took a cigarette each and lit up. After taking a few puffs, Jude began, "It has been some time since, we have come out of jail now. I am getting itchy feet again." Charlie smiled, "Mate, I am not missing those heavy shackles around my legs and I like the comfort of my warm bed. But I do not know if I will be able to keep it up for long though. Money is a very fickle and elusive mistress."

Leo looked at both of them intently. "Guys, I did not bring you all the way out here to look pretty. I have been working on my plan. I have not made much progress though". Jude answered eagerly, "Whatever it is Leo, I am in. Just tell us what needs to be done" Leo looked at Charlie who replied, "Well it's the same with me Leo." Jude next asked Leo about their other mates, "But what about Samuel and Frank?" Charlie looked at Leo in enquiry as well. Leo answered, "They need to pitch in as well. I wonder if they will be joining us today".

Jude is now very eager. "So, what have you been cooking Leo?" Leo laughed. "I am planning on us robbing the ECC bank." Charlie was open mouthed. He said, "You know Leo that the security in that bank is very tight!" Leo answered calmly, "Yes I know Charlie, but there is no fun if a job is too easy." Jude and Charlie looked at each other and then at Leo. Jude was the first one to break the silence. "So, tell us what is the plan," Leo sighed wearily, "There is no plan at the moment, Jude. I have been watching the bank for the past week and I know that it is heavily guarded during the day. It is also a very busy bank" He continued, "However, in the evening; the alarm is set, the lights in the foyer are turned on and then everyone goes home. The rest of the office is in darkness and not visible from the outside. We need to know the lay out of the bank from the inside and come up with something that is fool proof and can be done in the evening."

Jude looked at Leo carefully, "Leo, you have always been the leader. Why are you so down in the dumps now?" Leo answered, "Jude, I am getting a little bit sick of going to the prison again and again. I just want to do something big and then settle down for a good while." Jude answered him, "I know Leo, I have the same feeling but there is no point in you getting steeped in misery. We will be useless after that." Leo smiled, "Okay pal, I will remain cheerful."

Leo kept his tea cup down. He thought for a while. Charlie asked him, "How much do you think is in there?" Leo smiled at him and answered, "Approximately twenty-million Euros, Charlie! Will that be enough for you?" He looked at Charlie's amazed face. He then began, "Okay Jude, first of all, we will go and stake the bank out properly from the inside and then make a plan. You begin with the job tomorrow." Jude answered, "Can I do something else?" Jude looks at Leo's face and reconsiders, "It is a boring job but yes it will be done."

Leo became very annoyed, "I hope no one grumbles after this about the nature of the jobs. We do not have the luxury to be choosy. A job cannot be done well if the ground work is not laid out properly. And, I don't really like people who whine." Both Jude and Charlie keep quiet. Leo continued, "I will take over from you in the afternoon." Charlie and Samuel bid goodbye to Leo at the door and walked outside. It is now late evening and the sun was hanging low on the horizon. A smattering of clouds were, tinged with the golden hue of the setting sun.

Samuel is walking with his hands deep in his pockets. His head is bent down in thought. Charlie looked at him and wondered what the problem was. He asked Samuel, "Are you all right, Sam? Are you worried about what Leo said to you?" Samuel did not respond. Charlie continued, "I know; Leo is rude at times--" Samuel turned around to look at Charlie and admonished him harshly, "shut up Charlie. Leo is correct, we have no right to complain. If we don't do the job carefully, we will all end up in prison." He further continued, "I am thinking about how to come with a plan to stake out the bank. I am not thinking about Leo." Charlie now keeps quiet. They continue to walk in silence.

****

In the morning, Samuel went into the bank as a courier person. He went to the customer service and handed over the parcel. He waited for the staff to sign the docket. He begins to hum to himself and looked around while he was waiting. There was a total of five cameras. Five counters for the day to day business; five foreign exchange counters and two international transaction cubicles. The staff signed the docket and handed it back to Samuel. The security guard on each door; looked carefully at Samuel as he passed them by. He went out to the delivery van, got in on the driving seat; he closed the door and drove away from the bank.

The young man who was sitting in the passenger seat was bound by his hands and legs to the seat. His mouth was stuffed with a cloth and taped. He was terrified. Samuel looked at him as he drove the van. He smiled menacingly at him. After driving for a while, he stopped the van in a deserted area. He then got out of the van and went around to the other side. He removed the tape and the cloth from the young man's mouth. He was gasping for air, “Please, please don't kill me” he pleaded. Samuel quietened him down with a shush. “Shut up. I am not going to kill you” and then he untied the young man. He handed him back his name badge and warned him, “So Harry, I am not going to kill you; but I have seen your address in the driving license. If you even ever breathe about this to anyone;

I will seek you out and kill you. Is that understood?" Harry nodded his head tearfully. Samuel patted him on the back, "Good lad. Now get going or you will be late." Harry scrambled into the driver seat and accelerated out of there. It was not a smooth and confident driving which is usually the case with most of the seasoned drivers. He was driving in a panic. Samuel laughed when the van hit the curb twice in Harry's haste.

Next day, Frank went into the bank. He waited for his turn in the queue. He looked around the bank as if he was passing his time. He can see motion detector cameras in the four corners of the hall and one in the center. When he was ready to be served, he took out twenty-thousand Polynesian Franc notes from his pocket and his driving license. He asked for the Euro equivalent of the currency.

The woman inspected the bundle of note and the driving License. She then rang the buzzer on the wall. In a few minutes, another lady came out of the inner chamber. “Yes, Maria!” The lady, Maria turned to look at the woman who arrived. “Jennifer, this gentleman here needs five thousand euros in place of these Polynesian Francs”. Jennifer looked at the driver's license that Maria handed over to her. She then looked at Frank. “Excuse me sir, we will have to get this money from the safe. This is a large amount. Hope you don't mind waiting for a few minutes. Usually we need some notice for a large amount”. She looked at him up and down.

Frank cleared his throat and spoke "Thank you ma'am. I was not aware. I am sorry." He smiled charmingly at them. Jennifer smiled back. Maria and Jennifer left him standing at the counter and went into the inner chamber of the bank.

Maria came back after a few minutes, she was carrying a bundle of fifty Euro notes in her hands. She counted out the money in Frank's presence and handed it over to him in an envelope. "All the best sir" Frank smiled again, "Thanks ma'am, now I can travel around without having to nip into the bank on and off." He mock saluted her and left the counter. He was whistling softly as he walked out of the door of the bank.

Today, Samuel was in the bank and he was waiting in the queue to the ATM. A lady came out from the office behind the teller. She looked at a man who had been waiting for a very long time. "Hello sir, my name is Jennifer. I am very sorry for the delay. It is a very busy day because of the year end. How can I help you today?" The man answered, "I just want to open my locker." Jennifer smiled, "Thank you for waiting. I will ask my colleague to join me and then we can go." The man nodded his head. He was annoyed as he was going to be late for the gala evening, he was supposed to go with his wife. Jennifer looked at Maria and indicated to her to join her. Maria signaled that she is coming and then she concluded the business she was doing for another customer. Samuel watched all of this and stored it in his memory.

****

A week had passed by since they got the orders from Leo. Thankfully Leo was a very patient type and will not begin a job until he was convinced that everyone involved in the preparation is ready. Samuel was now sitting in a car which is parked on the street parking outside ECC bank. He was waiting for one particular car to come out of the basement car park of the bank. Samuel was given the responsibility of staking out the two women and find out about their transportation. Charlie does not know how to drive any vehicle and he was suffused with alcohol most of the time now. It will only bring more trouble if he did something major. He was only allowed to do simple tasks.

After a few minutes had passed, he saw Jennifer's car coming out of the basement and turning left on the street. She was driving at a snail's pace because of the traffic. Once she had a few minutes lead, Samuel got into the lane behind her. She took the highway after a while and increased the speed.

He carefully drove his car in the same lane and overtook several cars at various points. Now, his car was directly behind hers. It looked like she was traveling in the direction of Epsom. It will be a good while, before the destination will arrive. He settled himself for the long drive after lighting a cigarette. The air coming in through the open window was nice and crisp.

Jennifer overtook a few cars and then slid back into the slow lane. Samuel continued at the same speed and did not bother to get any closer. There will be an exit shortly. If she took that exit and he didn't, he will lose her. It had been a good few days since Leo had given him this job. He had tried very hard to follow her and had lost her one way or the other. "Here comes the exit to Epsom," he mumbled to himself. "I am ready for you this time; my darling."

But Jennifer kept driving. "Strange!" he thought to himself. He had lost her here somewhere yesterday. The car kept speeding. Soon a filling station appeared in the far horizon. Jennifer indicated and then turned into the parking lot of the filling station. "So, this is where I missed you yesterday my love!" Samuel thought to himself. He waited in the parking lot about four cars on the left of Jennifer's car and behind. He waited for a good few minutes.

Eventually Jennifer came out of the building with two young beautiful girls in tow. They were holding their mother's hand on either side and skipping as they walked to keep up with her. Both were talking to their mother in loud animated voices. They had their back packs on their back; probably school bags. The two front teeth were missing in the one girl's mouth. "Eight or nine years, the other one is probably six" calculated Samuel.

Jennifer ensured that the girls sat down in the car properly and belted up. She then drove out of the car park and was back on the highway within minutes. She now took the exit to Leather head. Frank continued to follow their until Jennifer pulled into a drive way.

The house was beside River Mole and was located on a high rise to prevent flood waters from reaching the house. It was a huge villa and looked Edwardian in design. Once they reached the drive, the girls opened the door and ran to the house as soon as the car came to a stop. The door of the house opened. An elderly lady came and stood at the doorway. She had a big smile on her face. "Nanny!" the two girls pelted to her. She spread both her arms wide and gathered them into her bosom. Jennifer was smiling as she locked the door and walked into the house.

Samuel drove on after observing this interaction. The women had gone in and closed the door after them. He took a right turn at the next junction and drove back to the vicinity of her house. The front of the house opened to a small lane, but the back of the house backed out in to the woods. The nearest house was at least five hundred meter away, "This is good, assuming that the land surrounding the Ward's house belonged to them; they are pretty isolated," he thought to himself. He looked around the perimeter. It was dark, although there were many cars still driving by. He parked beside a tree and took out the binocular. He looked around the space behind their home. He could see a barn, stables, well maintained lawns and a large kitchen garden. He turned the binocular towards the house and focused it on one of the windows on the ground floor.

It looked like he was looking into the large kitchen. The girls were seated at the smaller table and were doing their homework with intense concentration. Their grandmother was sitting beside them and knitting something. Jennifer was bustling around in the kitchen preparing dinner. After putting together whatever she was cooking, she kept it in the oven and came and sat beside her mother with two cups.

The large dinner table was already set. On the side board were bottles of wine, wine glasses and bowls full of snacks of various kinds. In a while, Frank heard the sound of another car come up the drive. He understood from looking through the lens, that the people in the house also could hear it. The girls looked up and then ran out of the kitchen.

In a few minutes, the girls came back with two people. One was a tall burly man with greyish hair and the other one was a tall man in his forties. The young girl was sitting on the shoulder of the older man. Frank began to make assumptions. "That is grand-daddy, I suppose. Then the other one has to be the father. They probably all live in the same household." In a few hours, his theory was confirmed. They all sat down to dinner. The older lady took out the salad bowl from the fridge. The younger man brought the tray out of the oven. The older man carved the meat and Jennifer handed around plates served with piping hot potatoes. Samuel's tummy began to grumble loudly from hunger. The family ate their food after saying grace.

An hour after dinner, the older couple got up with the children and walked up to the stairs that were visible beside the kitchen. The night time activities came alive on second floor. Meanwhile Jennifer and her husband were sitting on the couch in the living room with a glass of wine each. Samuel waited till all the lights were turned out in the house.

"Nothing more to learn for tonight" he surmised. He then slowly eased his car out from behind the tree and rolled it down the slope with the engine turned off. Noise carries for a long distance in the country side, especially at night. He then slowly turned the ignition of his car when he could not roll it any further. At least, he was some distance away from the house now.

****

Next day at around three in the evening, Frank went to the petrol station past the exit to Epsom; and filled up the car tank. He then went inside to pay for the fuel. He visited the restroom and sat in the cubicle for a while. He came out after spending some time in there. He then ordered some food from the deli and sat down to eat it in the seating area.

Although he was busy eating, his eyes were glued to the road. Samuel had handed over details of what he had to look out for. A car pulled up and parked in the reserved space. Frank's face now lit up with excitement. The grandfather had parked the car and the two girls ran in. Samuel had described the family perfectly. They had their school bags with them. Their father came out of the office to receive them. They ran up to him and hugged him. The four of them walked back in. Frank continued to sit there and watch.

He had finished his lunch. Now he purchased a cup of coffee and he took his time savoring the aroma and flavor. Jennifer walked in exactly at four O' clock. The girls came out with their grandfather. Jennifer kissed the old man on the cheek. She then left with the girls after they had waved good bye to their granddad. Frank smiled and thought to himself, “So this is the stopover between home and school. The men work here or probably own the place”. More likely latter, judging by the size of their house and the thoroughbred horses, Samuel had seen in the barn. They could afford to send the girls to a private school. There was a famous private school nearby. Jennifer while returning from work, picked them up and brought them back home. The grandmother stayed at home and minded the house and the animals.

****

In the meantime, Jude was following Maria. He had learnt a lot about her in a short space of time. First was the fact that Maria lived on her own in a house in Croydon. The bank was only fifteen minutes by car from her living quarters; however commuted by the train daily. "Wise choice" Jude thought to himself. She had an on and off boyfriend who sometimes stayed the night. Jude knew exactly when this happened. It was Tuesdays and Wednesdays on not all, but some of the weeks. To him it looked like he flew in from somewhere. It was the chauffeur driven car from the airlines that dropped him off. He didn't stay the whole night either. She could very well be his mistress. That explained the irregular visits and the short stay. A shared dinner and possibly a quick tumble in the bed. He then left in a preordered taxi.

Every day after returning home from the bank she changed into her running gear. She ran five miles daily and then returned. Ten miles in total! She then gets changed into her tennis gear and comes out of the house in thirty minutes. Meanwhile she would have made herself a cup of coffee. She does look very sexy in that gear! She goes to the tennis club and plays tennis for an hour. She comes back to the house after purchasing ready to cook meals from the local butcher. It seems like she pays up front for her supply. The butcher has the brown bag always ready for her while everyone else will usually wait for their purchase. Once back in the house, she puts the pack in the oven. Then she pours out a glass of red wine and lets it breathe. In the meanwhile, she reads a magazine or a novel. She then sits down for dinner. Half an hour if the boyfriend is not there; an hour if he is in. It is as if she is trying to prolong his stay.

Once dinner is over, she will watch television for a little while. She then goes into her bedroom and flicks a few magazines or continues to read the unfinished novel. This week she was reading a novel by Clive Dev called 'True Colors, the accidental heist'. Jude had got a closer look at the title while she was reading it on the train. Lights were always switched off at ten at night. A very disciplined life for the weekdays!

The weekend was a total contrast. She was out in the pub dancing on both Friday and Saturday night. No workout, no decorum and totally drunk! She slept through all of Sunday and then became the well behaved, golden girl on Monday morning.

****

The men had been following these two women for a whole month. They now knew exactly how, the two of them spent almost every minute of their life. They knew their families and their activities as well. They were ready to get into action. They were going to meet Leo at his house this evening. Samuel who is in the supermarket; is buying various types of beer and some bites, a pack of cigarettes and some mint gums. He comes out of the shop and gets into his car. He then drove to Leo's house. The minute he had parked the car, Charlie came out of the house and helped Samuel to carry the bag into the house. "Hello Samuel, let me give you a hand with that bag." Samuel grinned, "Thanks mate". He smiled to himself when he noticed that Charlie picked up the bag with the beers. They both went into the house and kept the drinks and snacks on the table. Leo smiled at Samuel, "Thanks mate for offering to keep us well watered." Samuel laughed, "I hope Charlie leaves enough for us to even wet our lips." Charlie acted as if he was offended. But his eyes were smiling. "Promise boys, I'll let you dip your fingers." They all laughed with gusto. Leo told Samuel that, Frank was on his way. "He is buying us some food." Samuel answered, "That's great leader. We will eat, drink and make merry". Leo answered, "Yes that is all right; but this is not a party. We have to make plans". The doorbell thankfully rang at the exact moment which saved Samuel from responding. Leo looked out from behind the curtains and then opened the door. Jude and Frank walked in with five paper bags full of food. The mouth-watering aroma of Indian food wafted in the room. They kept the food packets on the table and sat down on the chairs. The room was sparse. This was only a temporary abode where Leo was living for a short while. Once they robbed the bank, they will be out of here in a flash. The men sat down around the chairs, ate the food and drank the beer while making plans.

****

On the evening of the 21st, of January, Leo, Frank and Jude drove to the River Lane where Jennifer lived. It was a very dark evening. The thick fog forced the visibility level down to zero. The fog warning could be heard periodically on the radio. Most people were staying indoors. The weather was predicted to become worse overnight. The animals were all herded into the barn from the pastures by the young lad that came to work for the household. He had gone home soon afterwards. The men sat waiting at the spot beside the tree, which Samuel had earlier chosen for surveillance. Leo was relaying all of the activities unfolding in the house; as he was seeing them occur with the help of the binocular.

Meanwhile, Samuel and Charlie had gone and parked outside the bank in the street parking. It was almost six and Jennifer had not left the bank. They were both getting anxious. Leo was, already informed about this. But he had asked them to stay put. His argument was that they had seen her going to work in the morning and the men had taken turns all day to watch the bank. She had not left the bank at all. At around six o' clock, Jennifer's car and a few other cars, come out of the basement of the bank. She headed towards the exit. Samuel now informed Leo of the latest developments and began to follow her. Leo answered, “Maybe it was a meeting or something”.

While they were waiting near the tree, the male members of Jennifer's household had arrived from the petrol station. They went into their various rooms as opposed to sitting at the dinner table just like every other night. "What's going on? There is a change in their timetable today" Leo said aloud. "What change?" asked Frank. "They are not sitting down for dinner as they do normally. They have all gone into their rooms". He thought for a few seconds. Leo came to a decision very quickly. "let's wait and see what they are up to. We can improvise accordingly".

In a few minutes, the grandfather appeared out of his bedroom followed by granny. They were immaculately dressed in their fineries. The granny was sparkling with a set of Jewellery with huge pearls. "Must have cost a fortune!" Leo relayed to the others. The children came out next and then their father. "Looks like they are all going somewhere". Jude panicked and asked, "Are we cancelling our schedule?" Leo answered sharply, "No we are not. Unexpected things will always happen. We should be prepared for every contingency!"

Leo looked at Frank. He said, "Yo Frank, turn on your cell phone and stay connected; follow them to where ever they are going. When you reach the place, let me know. I will tell you what to do next at that point." Frank answered, "Okay Leo, but you don't have a car to get away." Leo answered calmly, "That should not be a problem; we can use Jennifer's car when she gets here". Frank knew that Leo's mind was made up. Without saying another word, he opened the car door. He got in and rolled his car down the hill. He went and parked behind a few bushes outside Jennifer's house. Once the family car came out and took the exit, he followed them. He gave them a few minutes lead. Because of the weather condition, they were driving slowly. Traffic was now very sparse as well. He could not go any closer. He stayed behind them at a distance and tailed them. The car turned into a church building in the village and parked. Frank drove past and then came back to the church and parked his car beside theirs. Few other cars were parked outside as well. He sat there for a few minutes and then got out of the car. He walked to the main hall and the altar. It was empty. He genuflected with reverence in front of the altar and went around to the side of the church. He went and looked at a few windows that opened into the other rooms of the building. He kept his head low. He did not find anyone in any of the rooms.

At the very end of the building, there was another long hall. Soft noise and music could be heard coming out of this place. Frank carefully looked in through one of the glass windows. There were about twenty people sitting around a very handsomely decorated dinner table. Frank could see that Jennifer's family was also sitting at the same table. He cautiously walked away from there. He went back and sat in his car. He called Leo on the mobile phone. “Yo Leo, it looks as if some kind of dinner is going on. More than likely a rehearsal dinner”. Leo thought for a good while. He said to him, “Frank, the children are also present; so more than likely it will be only until eight or nine. Stay there and watch; I will call you back." Leo then swiped the phone to disconnect the line.

He thought for a few more minutes and then called Samuel. Charlie answered at the first ring as he was holding the phone in his hands. Leo asked, "Samuel, where are you?" Charlie answered, "We are on the highway tailing Jennifer." Leo answered back, "Okay stay close to her. Where do you think she is headed?" Samuel answered as he could hear them speaking on the speaker phone, "Looks like she is headed home, why?" He did not respond to that. There was no time. He had to decide what to do next. "Have you entered the village yet?" he asked the two of them. "No," answered Samuel. Leo thought for a few minutes and then replied, "Okay stay close and call me if she drives past the church in the village and heads home. If not, call me from wherever she goes." Samuel agreed and disconnected his phone. Charlie looked at him in enquiry and then shook his head, "Just very like Leo. Can he not explain what was happening?" Samuel looked at Charlie, "Maybe he does not know yet, as to how this is going to unfold" Charlie looked at Samuel as if he could not understand.

Samuel explained to him patiently as if he were saying it to a five year old boy!. "See Charlie, according to our plan, we were going to kidnap the whole family and threaten them. It is difficult to stick to the play; when the actors have no clue about their role. Say for example, Jennifer was late coming out of the bank today of all days. May be something changed at the other end too and that is why Leo is asking us to tell him what he wants to know. He will explain it to us when he knows it himself." Charlie looked out to the road. It was pitch dark but, the church tower called to them like a beacon. "I can see the church spire in the distance." Samuel answered, "Okay, keep an eye on her car". Jennifer meanwhile, looked at the church as she was driving past; but she did not go in. She kept on driving towards the house which was now only five minutes away. Samuel called Leo and let him know. He asked Samuel to bring his car into the church and join Frank. Samuel did a right turn at the next exit and drove back to the church. He pulled in beside Frank's car. They both got out and joined Frank in his car. Frank relayed to Samuel and Charlie, what had happened so far.

Jennifer had by now got out of the car and opened the door to the house. The light was left on in the corridor. She went into the living room and switched on the light. She was surprised to see a man; a stranger sitting on the couch. She opened her mouth to scream but a hand clamped her mouth from the back and stuck a gun to her flank, just adjacent to her kidney. "Hello Jennifer," said the man who was seated on the couch. "We are here expecting you to co-operate. In exchange we will give you back your family". Jennifer smiled. Leo indicated to Jude to remove his hand from her mouth. Jude did so after cautioning her, "One word and your kidney will explode. Is that understood?" Jennifer nodded. Jude let go of his hand from her mouth. Jennifer answered with some pride in her voice,

“You are lying. My family is not here”. Leo got up menacingly from the couch.

He brought his face very close to Jennifer's and looked at her with daggers in his eyes. He practically hissed at her, “How dare you call me a liar? At this moment, your family is in the village church enjoying the rehearsal dinner”. He paused and allowed time for the message to sink in. He then continued, “My men are waiting outside. A whole crowd will stop short at the point of a gun. They have one each in their both hands. There are only twenty of your people in there, that too without any weapon! Do you know how to do the math?” Jennifer's eyes were now panicking in fear. Leo looked at her face, “Good. I can see that you now, very well understand the gravity of your situation," he smiled at her.

Jennifer was in shock. She did not know what to say. Leo continued, "If you are willing to co-operate; then we can continue this conversation further." Jennifer literally begged, "I will do anything you want. Just leave my family alone". Leo looked at her carefully. "Okay, I will spare your family; if you help us to rob your bank." Jennifer was extremely terrified now. Her eyes were wide with horror. "You know, I can't do that? I will lose my job." Leo took out a coin from his breast pocket. He tossed it in his hand and looked at it. He replied coolly but with sarcasm in a high pitched voice as if imitating Jennifer. "Heads or tails? Oh heads! Fine you can keep your job, but you will lose your family. Is that all right with you?"

Jennifer was very confused now. These men were serious. They will not stop at anything. She has to change tactics. "look, I want to keep my family safe, but I can't ---------" Her words trailed away when Leo completed it for her, "Yes I know that you can't open the safe on your own Jennifer. You need Maria with you." Jennifer's eyes became wide open with surprise. Her pupils were completely dilated in fear. "How do you know all of this?" Then she thought to herself, "What a stupid question? Obviously, they have done their homework."

Leo continued to look at her for a few seconds. He was trying to read her facial expression. He knew that she was nearly at breaking point. Leo ordered her. "You will ring Maria and tell her that you are going to her house and that you need to speak to her. Is that understood?" Jennifer nodded. Leo then handed over the mouth piece of the land line phone to her. Jude stuck the gun further into her back. She cried in pain. "Please don't. It hurts badly. Am I not doing what you have asked me to do?" Jude replied in a threatening voice, "This is a warning to you to not do any mischief while you are on the phone. Remember your family." Jennifer was exasperated. "What am I going to say to her though?" Leo smiled, "Don't worry dear sister, I will tell you what to say to her."

Jennifer dialled Maria's phone number. Maria answered at the second ring. "Hello, who is this?" Jennifer could hear heavy breathing on the other side of the line. She said, "Maria, this is Jennifer. This is the number for my land line. Sorry to disturb you while you are on your daily jog. I want to speak to you. Can I call over now?" Maria frowned, thought for a while and asked, "Can it not wait until tomorrow?" Jennifer emphatically answered, "No Maria, I have discovered something about my husband. I feel that I cannot go to anyone else with this. I want to speak to you urgently."

Maria heard the panic in Jennifer's voice. Her own breathing has slowed down by now. She answered, "Okay Jennifer, I will be back in my house in ten to fifteen minutes. If you start now, you will reach approximately at the same time." Jennifer thanked her and disconnected the phone. She looked at the men. Leo nodded, "Okay we are going to take your car. I will drive and you will be a nice company to this handsome gentleman. Any mischief and you are dead meat, Don't worry! We will send your family to keep you company in heaven as well. Do you agree?" Jennifer nodded her head. They came out of the house cautiously and got into the car. He then rang Frank, "I have the package. Just keep the family busy. If I tell you to go ahead, shoot all of them. Is that okay?" Jennifer screamed into the phone. "No please don't do that. I will do as I am told." All the men including Frank, Samuel and Charlie at the other end; laughed at Jennifer's distress.

The weather had turned for the worse now. Leo drove the car while Jude sat at the back and kept an eye on Jennifer. He had the gun sticking into her ribs. The rain had stopped but the road was very slippery and wet. Leo was taking his time driving and was being extra careful. Jennifer's car was a sports model. It ate up the kilometers in minutes. They reached Maria's house within ten minutes; but Leo brought the car to a halt at the side near a bend on the road. He turned the headlights down. They waited. "Why are we stopping here? Why are we not going to Maria's house? What about my family?" Jennifer cried. Leo calmly replied, "Have some patience sister. We know what to do. Your family is fine for now. They will be safe as long as you don't act funny."

They can now see Maria running on the footpath. She reaches her house and gets in. She turns on the light in the living room. Leo now edged the car closer to Maria's house but not in to the drive. He got out of the car and hid behind the bushes by the side of the house. Jude walked behind Jennifer; with the gun still pointed at her back. They both reached the front door. Jude hid behind the side wall; but Jennifer could see his gun clearly. She looked at him in terror. He indicated with the gun to her to get moving. He had a menacing look in his eyes. Jennifer moved closer to the door and rang the doorbell. She waited with bated breath for a few minutes. Now she could hear footsteps on the inside. Maria opened the door and smiled at Jennifer. “Come in Jennifer. What took you so long? I thought you were in a hurry!” she turned around to walk in.

Leo who was waiting for this opportunity, came out from behind the bushes and appeared at the front door. Maria's back was turned to him. He stepped in on the door step and clamped on Maria's mouth tightly from behind. With one swift movement, he turned Maria around effortlessly. Although Jennifer was expecting it and had decided to interfere, it happened so quickly that she had no time to react. Maria looked at Jennifer in shock and anger. She apologised to Maria in a tearful voice, "I am so sorry" Jude screamed at her through clenched teeth, "Shut up and sit down in the car quickly; otherwise, I will blow her head off." Jennifer got inside the car as quickly as she could.

Leo pushed Maria in to the inside of the car and closed the door on that side. Jude waited for Leo to start the car and simultaneously closed the door. Leo applied the automatic lock. He did not want a dead woman to foil his plans. They may be tempted to jump out. Jude meanwhile had got into the passenger seat in front. He kept the gun at a low level but, pointed at the two of them now. Leo began to drive and now they were on their way to the bank. "Maria, welcome aboard" said Leo. Maria looked at him searchingly. She did not recognise him. She looked at Jennifer inquiringly. Leo, who was watching all this in the rearview mirror continued. "Oh, not to worry! Jennifer is not part of this. Her family has been held hostage by my men. You just have to help me rob the bank". He looked at Maria and then continued, "If you don't; needless to say, that her family will be killed. But it will also be your last day on Earth". Maria absorbed all of this, "How do you know that we are responsible for the vault?" She asked in exasperation.

Leo laughed, “That my love in the cop's language; is called Surveillance!” Maria asked, “Are you the police?” Leo laughed again, “No we are their other half’s. You know cops and robbers? I am sure you have played the game in your childhood. We are that half, the robbers, ha ha ha.”

****

By this time, they had reached the bank. Leo drove into the basement of the car park. He parked the car at a blind spot where it will not be picked up by any of the cameras. He does not mind the car being seen. It was Jennifer's car, but their faces should not be recorded. He was careful of that. The four of them walked up to the exit lift. The men had turned their faces away from the camera. They made the women go in to the lift first, then they asked them to turn around to face them. They then took cover by the women's torso shielding them from the camera. Then they straightened and stood up. Jude managed to keep his gun pointed at them through all of this.

The lift regurgitated them on the fourth floor. Leo looked around while Jude kept an eye on the women. There were no cameras in this room but, he was sure that some of them were probably hidden near the safe. Leo asked them, "How many cameras are here?" Both of them kept quiet. They falsely assumed that the men will be deterred by the thoughts of the camera. Jude dug deep into Jennifer's back with his gun. Jennifer hastily said, "There are two cameras in the room where the vault is". Jude jeered, "Now, was that so hard to answer?" Maria looked at him in disgust. Leo asked them the details of the vault. Jennifer explained that there was a combination code to the lock and then Maria and Jennifer both had to use their thumb print for the scanner. He replied casually, "Get on with it then ladies. I don't want to be here the whole night. Jennifer, I am sure that you want to get back to your family?" Jennifer hastily stepped forward. She beseeched Maria with her eyes. Maria stood there stubbornly. Jude prodded her with the gun to help her decide.

Leo shouted at them, "Shut down the cameras and open up fast both of you." Maria and Jennifer together proceeded to open up the safe. Leo looked at them. He commanded, "Lie down on the ground now with your hands behind your head." They both did likewise. Luke indicated to Jude; who stood behind them and positioned his gun directly above their head. Luke went into the vault and stuffed a few large bags with money, gold bars and Jewellery. He came out of the vault with four overloaded bags and asked them to get up. "Now close the vault. No tricks. If I hear the police siren, I will kill you both". Jennifer and Maria both closed the door of the vault together. Leo and Jude took the bags and hung them cross wise on both their shoulders. Now Leo also brought his own gun out. They pushed the women forward and followed them to the basement. The poor women were terrified. They have the money now but, that was no guarantee that these men will let them live! Together the group walked to the car and the women got bundled in. Jennifer again asked them to let her family go; now that they have the money. "Patience little sister, patience" said Luke. Jennifer bit her lips in anxiety.

****

They drove out of the bank and out of the city. Once they reached the highway; Leo called Samuel on his mobile, "Cash secure. Are you ok? What about the family?" Samuel answered that they were all still inside. Leo replied happily, "Okay then you can leave from there and we will meet at the agreed spot. Over and out." He turned to look at Jennifer, "Your family is fine. They are no longer a hostage, but you girls still are. So, continue to behave." He looked at Maria and said, "You are lucky that you don't have a family living with you here". Leo gave them a stern warning and drove the car for a good while. A few recognisable land marks passed by. Eventually he reached an isolated spot on the highway and took an exit road. He drove further till he reached a wooded area. He stopped the car on the side of the road. Jude got down and got the girls out. "We are going to leave you here. You can find your own way back." Jennifer and Maria got out. But Jennifer protested, "You can't leave us here. What if someone else comes and does something? You will be guilty of the way our life turned out." Jude laughed, "Do we look like people who carry regret and remorse? What happens to you now is your problem."

He got into the car and looked back. "Adios ladies!" he saluted and closed the door on his side. Leo accelerated the car and they drove away. Jennifer and Maria both now look frustratingly at the receding tail light of the car. They had now nearly become the victims of the Stockholm syndrome.

****

Maria snapped out of it first. She looked sharply at Jennifer, "How dare you get us into this situation? Why did you bring them to my house? Now we will both look like thieves." Jennifer pleaded to Maria to calm down. When Maria did not show signs of stopping, Jennifer shouted. "Shut up Maria, they told me that they have been trailing us for one whole month. I have family so, they used them as leverage. If you had had any family, I would have been the one shouting at you. My situation is actually worse. Can you even see the irony of my situation? I know that my family has been held hostage, but they had no clue about the danger they were in. How does that make me look? Can you imagine what the police will think of me?"

Realization dawned on Maria. Her mouth was open like a gold fish. She hurriedly apologised to Jennifer, "I am sorry Jennifer. I did not realise." Jennifer pacified her, "No forget it, I would have been the same if our situations were reversed. Let's concentrate on getting help. We were on the highway and then he took the exit on the left. So, the town should be on the right. On our way here, I had seen the direction to the aquatic center on the right, so we are somewhere around Langleybury. Let us follow this road and see where it leads us. As any town goes;

there should be a filling station not too far away. Do you know what time it is?"

Maria shook her head in the negative. "I have no watch on me and there was no chance to pick up the cell phone." Jennifer sighed, "I had the mobile on my person, but they made me empty the pockets before they got me out of my house." She went on to relate the whole incidence to Maria. Maria now understood her friend's predicament. After they had walked for a good distance, they saw the sign board for a filling station. They took the road leading to it. By now Jennifer was limping. She was in her high heels from office. She was a horse rider and that was how she kept fit. Walking was not up her sleeve. She did try her level best to not slow them down.

Maria walked comfortably because she was wearing her runners and she had the stamina to walk. About an hour later, they saw the filling station at the distance. They looked at that beacon of hope and sighed with relief. Now they got the energy to walk faster. Soon they reached the filling station. Jennifer looked at the door and found that it was locked. She went to the shop window. A voice asked over the intercom "Ladies how can I help you?" Jennifer answered, "Sorry we need to use your phone." The male voice apologised, "Sorry ladies, company policy. We cannot open the door after six in the evening." Jennifer nodded her head in exasperation. Being the part owner of their own petrol station, she knew better than most.

The staff in the Epsom petrol station had always complained about people wanting to come inside. They always had one or other valid excuse, "Yes I know," she said with gritted teeth. "Can you at least call the emergency services and report a bank robbery?" she asked. The voice took its time answering, "Yes, I can do that." He rang the emergency services. The police asked him questions to which he had very little or no answers. Frustrated, the dispatch officer on duty asked the man to let the ladies in to the shop. "Can you please let them in? At least you have us on this end. If any problem, just shout; we will be there in no time." The man opened the door with the help of a remote switch and closed it as soon as they entered. "Please answer the officer's questions on the phone," he said with extreme displeasure. He was annoyed at his calm evening being destroyed. Moreover, the officer had jeered at him for calling in a bank robbery; he had no idea about. While Jennifer was on the phone to the police, Maria asked the man to let her use the rest room. Jennifer was off the phone; by the time she came out. They could now hear the wail of the sirens in the distance. Jennifer quickly used the toilet as she knew that, once the police got here; they will grill her for a long time!

Once the shop assistant realised that these women were not thieves and vandals, he made them a cup of coffee each and offered some buns, fruits and water to them. They gratefully took it from him. Jennifer asked his permission to use the phone to ring her family. Her husband sounded worried when he answered the phone.

Before he could say anything, Jennifer spoke, "Joseph, you all right?" Joseph was flabbergasted, "Jennifer, what is wrong? I am here worried about you not showing up for the rehearsal dinner and not answering your phone; you are asking me if I was all right?"

Jennifer quickly answered, "I am fine. I am in the filling station at Edgware. We were forced to help rob our bank". Joseph interrupted her on the other end. "sorry Maria and me were forced to help rob the bank at gun point----" She paused and listened carefully. She then answered, "No, no, no don't worry. We are safe now. How are mum, dad and Anna and Poppy?" Joseph answered, "They are fine. Albert and Grace went home with the children. I was waiting for you at the church for the after-dinner drinks. They rang back to say that they found your phone on the couch at home. What happened? Jennifer cut into the conversation, "I will tell you later, but the story in short is that I went home after our executive meeting to get ready and I was held at gun point. I am fine and unhurt. But the police are here now, and I have to get off the phone. I am here in the filling station in Edgware. Can you come here and I will tell you everything, You can also bring me home then. Just let mom know the minor details. Don't alarm them please!"

Jennifer kept the phone down and turned around to see a police officer and a paramedic waiting to speak to her. "Hello there, my name is Luke, a police constable and I have been dispatched to speak to you about the robbery. Could you tell me your name please?" asked the police officer. Jennifer took a deep breath, "My name is Jennifer Ward. Maria Logan and I are colleagues. We are employees of the ECC bank." Officer Luke kept taking notes as she spoke. He asked a few questions as necessary.

Meanwhile the paramedic had sat Jennifer down on a chair and was examining her leg. Her beautifully pedicured feet were covered in blisters; she had incurred from the long walk. He cleaned the blisters and dressed them in a soothing lotion. She had already given them the registration number of her car which was used for the getaway. She could hear the helicopter overhead scouring the area. "The men will be far away by now; they may be even out of the country," she thought.

****

The men however, were still in the country. They had no intention of leaving in a hurry. They had by now reached a place called Hempel Hampstead and were sitting inside a small cottage in a heavily wooded area. It was a hunting lodge and was empty. Leo had staked it out a few times. They were sitting around a fire with bottles of beer in their hand. The money was spread out on a rug in front of them in bundles of one hundred euros, gold bars and gold and silver Jewellery. Samuel counted the loot and split them in to five equal parts. He took a sip of beer and then put the money into five different gym bags. He did the same with the gold bars and the Jewellery.

Despite the loot being divided into five bags, they were extremely full. Samuel gave a bag to each one of them. First to Leo, "Here you go leader. Thank you for being the boss and completing the operation beautifully and successfully." Leo held up the beer bottle in acknowledgement and smiled. Samuel finished distributing the bags to everyone. Leo now said to them, "Listen up all of you. Use the ornaments first. When you get to mainland Europe, go to our regular place to dispose the gold bar. It will be a while before the money can be laundered. We are parting ways after this, and we won't talk to each other. Let the heat die down. You are all rich now; but spend the money wisely. Meet me at the end of May in Clive's Pub in Paris"

****

The National Crime Agency office is a big building in the middle of the city of London. It deals with organised crime in the United Kingdom and works with International partners from other countries mainly the countries of the European Economic Community. This office has solved a series of organised crimes related to drugs, money laundering, counterfeit money, child sex abuse and much more. The campus has many small buildings inside the walls and houses the different units.

In one such building is the department of Assets recovery and associated crimes. It is ten pm. Assistant police detective Veronica was sitting at her desk and typing some report into the computer. Her senior was sitting across from her on another table. His hands were locked behind his head. He was whistling away to himself. He was looking very pleased. He stopped whistling, sat down properly and looked at Veronica, "It took a long while to finish this case; at least it's over for now. We deserve a break." Veronica kept typing and smiled. She asked slyly, "So Dev, will I book tickets to Miami then?" Dev laughed.

Police constable Alex knocked on the door and came in at the same time. Dev looked at him and smiled, "What Alex, are you coming to Miami?" Alex initially balked in confusion. Then he solemnly replied, "Sir, I would love to, but this is not the right time." Veronica smiled, "Oh Alex, you are a spoil sport. You need to listen to yourself sometimes." Alex looked at Veronica as if he was looking at a small child. "I know miss. If people stop themselves from getting killed and people give up robbing banks, then I will stop spoiling your fun."

Dev sat up, "Did you say killed?" Alex turned to look at him and said patiently, "No sir, that was just an expression. But the control room just called. The ECC bank has been robbed and the victims were left stranded at the highway. They called it in from the Edgware petrol station. Luke is present at the scene." Dev is already busy strategising in his head. He looked at Alex, "What is the background story?" Alex told him what he knew about the incidence so far.

When Alex had finished speaking; Dev said, "If that is the case then there were more than two men. At least three, may be five.

The amount of money taken will tell us how many people were there. While the two were robbing the bank, the others were the look outs and were keeping the family hostage." He looked at the two of them, "Let's go and speak to the family. Luke can look after the women. Ask him to keep them at the station until we come back. Veronica asked, "What about the bank?" Alex answered, "A team has been dispatched already." Dev added, "The money and the men are gone. Close down the exits. Put extra men on patrol. Let the team continue. Ask the forensics to begin their work. We can go there after speaking to the victim and their family." Alex was confused. He asked, "But why visit the family?" Dev answered, "The testimony of the family and their body language will tell us if the women were involved in the plot and just playing the part of the damsel in distress".

****

Back in the hunting cottage, Jude asked Leo, "Where are you going to go Leo?" Leo answered, "It is better to not know about each other's whereabouts. We will vacate this cottage in the morning and will go our separate ways. Is that okay?" Everyone agreed to it. They sat up for long and had their drinks and food. They all went to sleep very late. It was not too late for them though. They were the professionals with night jobs!

Leo was the first one to wake up in the morning. Dawn was just breaking out in the East; but they had to leave. The police will have been looking for them the whole night.

He called out, “Wake up guys. We have to be out in fifteen minutes. Anyone interested in staying after that, will have to answer the police.” At the word 'police,' everyone got up and scrambled everywhere, the men were all ready to hit the road in ten minutes. Leo smiled at their prompt response. They left Jennifer's car beside the cottage and took their own two vehicles to escape. Leo went on his own. The other four took the one car and took a different exit once they were on the highway. They hooted their cars to wave goodbye. Leo nosed his car towards the county of Northampton. He could see the helicopter hovering overhead. “What are they doing here?” He thought to himself in irritation. “They should be looking at the ports”. He speculated that they were probably looking for Jennifer's car. “It won't be long before they find it". He had tried to mask the number as much as he could.

****

For Jennifer and Maria, the nightmare was not over until that afternoon. Her husband had come straight over to the filling station in Edgware, the previous night. He was not allowed to speak to her. He followed the patrol car in which his wife and Maria were taken to the police station like criminals. There also, he was not able to speak to her. Never in his life had he felt this sense of helplessness. Not even when Jennifer was giving birth at home! He was confident that, she was in the capable hands of the midwives. They were the experts that had mastered how to care for the woman during childbirth. He was a rich man and a big shot in the city. But he could not pull enough strings to even speak to his wife! A bank being robbed was a national offense and the victims were always the primary suspects. She and Maria were finally allowed to go home in the afternoon with a warning not to leave the city.

The CEO of ECC bank was there all morning with them. He was their pillar of strength. The knowledge that, he trusted his employees gave them consolation. Jennifer and Maria enjoyed great credibility with him. Jennifer's husband eventually brought her home in the afternoon and handed her over to the loving care of her mother. She strutted around Jennifer like a mother hen. She had heard the full news on the television and was terrified. They were not able to help the detectives that had questioned them. They had no clue that they were actually held hostages. The inspector who called himself Dev was a handsome and kind man. The first thing that he had done was to reassure her that her daughter was safe. She was glad that he thought of them as humans and not as a case. Jennifer had braved the perils for her family and kept them safe. Now it was her turn to care for her daughter.

****

The patrol car that was driving through the streets of Hempel Hampstead passed by the woods. The patrol officers had seen the car in the morning but thought that someone was using the cottage. Now it was early evening and the car was still there. They became curious. They had heard the bulletin about the bank robbery on the police transmitter. Now they were even more suspicious.

They drove silently into the woods and parked some distance away from the cottage. One of the policemen got out of the car and scouted the area. He approached the cottage on tip toe and looked in. He could not see anyone. He signaled to the other policeman who also got out of the police car. The number plate was dirty making it difficult to decipher them. He went closer and looked at the plate. It was covered in mud. He was torn between saving the evidence and not crying 'wolf'. He made an executive decision. There will be finger prints and more evidence inside the car. It was more important to check if their suspicion was actually correct.

He wiped the plate and checked the number. It matched the number of the car mentioned in the bulletin. He went back to the car radio and called in the sighting of the car, "Officer Theo reporting. The getaway car has been located in Hempel Hampstead by the hunting lodge in the wooded area. The cottage is empty".

****

Alex walked into the office. Dev looked up from the report he was reading. Alex said to Dev, "The bank manager Jennifer's car has been called in by Officer Theo. But there are no prints." Dev sighed, "You know Alex, for once I am inclined to agree with Veronica. You definitely bring bad news for me all the time. How can they leave no prints? People who did not bother to mask their faces will have left plenty of clues”. He sighed and stood up, “Okay let's go". Alex could not help himself replying, “No disrespect sir, but you will be bored without me. Veronica will make your life miserable by asking for trips abroad”. Veronica cleared her throat as an indication to Alex that she was not impressed. She logged out of the computer and got up. Alex drove the car and Dev sat beside him. Veronica got into the back seat. They drove to the wooded area in Hempel Hampstead and got out of their car.

Luke has already cordoned the scene and was looking on at the forensic experts who were taking samples. Dev went into the building. He looked around. There was a lot of empty bottles, cigarette butts, food and clothes. The forensic experts were working quietly. Dev asked Luke, "What time did you get here?" Luke answered, "The officer called it in at four this evening. I was here at five past four." He further explained that Theo had seen the car in the morning, but he thought that the hunters were using the lodge. The cottage belonged to the Smith family and they usually come during the weekend. But when the car was still there at four and he saw the make and the model, he was suspicious."

Luke signaled Theo to come close. Dev asked Theo, "So there was nothing yesterday evening here?" Theo answered, "Yes sir, I know the Smiths. When they come; they come in a group of four or five but only, after eight in the evening. They hunt at midnight. They stay in the lodge and allow the carcass to bleed overnight.

They then leave the lodge for their house around midday. The car was still here at four, that is why I decided to stop and check it out". Dev replied, "Good work officer. They may have left the country by now, but this is a good place to start."

The forensic officer approached Dev. He said, "The shoe print found at the bank, the Ward's residence and here, match provisionally. We just need to confirm it in the lab. What is more interesting is that there are more than four or five shoe prints? Also, there are three different tire marks and" Dev concludes the officer's sentence, "one tire mark belongs to Jennifer's car. So, there were four or more people who got away in two cars." Dev contemplated for a while. He then speaks aloud his speculation, "So after the bank robbery, they dropped the women off on the main road and came and hid here. They then divided their loot, had a good time and dispersed from here in two cars. This is a heavily wooded area, so the helicopter lights were not able to penetrate through last night. I wonder who they are and where they went from here?"

****

After separating from the group, it was evening when Leo hit the town of Crosspool near Sheffield. He went into a Chinese take away and ordered some noodles and chips. He went back to his car and sat down. He was voracious by now. He had not eaten all day. He devoured his food with gusto. The sweet and sour taste of the sauce woke his taste buds up. He did not stop eating until all the food was empty; not even a prawn cracker was left. Not satisfied, he licked the container with his fingers and finished off by licking his own fingers. He sighed with content. He could have been out of the country by now. He could have gone to mainland Europe but that was not his style. There was a score to settle as well. He was not a coward. He wanted to give someone particular in the police; some time and a good run for their money. He had heard the news on the radio. He had also heard that neither Jennifer nor Maria were able to remember their faces. He remarked to himself, "Are we that plain or could they not genuinely remember our faces in their fear?"

He began to drive again. He needed a place to stay for the night. It was too late to turn up to a bed and breakfast. He could probably sleep in the car. It wasn't too bad.

But he will have to pull in somewhere secluded. The Peak District National park was nearby. He decided to go there and stay the night. As he was reaching a roundabout, he saw a prostitute standing waiting in anticipation of potential customers. Leo slowed the car and pulled the window down, "Hi what is your name?" he asked. She smiled with her recently whitened teeth, "Clara! Interested?" Leo nodded his head and answered, "Yes, there is a wooded area back there. What do you think?" Clara continued to smile with a pouting lip. "If the money is right; why not?" Leo smiled, "Hop in then." She got into the car with graceful movements. He was in a hurry now. He drove to the edge of the wood near Crosspool and stopped the car. He turned off the lights and turned towards her.

They kept quiet but their bodies spoke to each other. After the carnal desires were met; Leo got out of the car to relieve himself in the woods. His back was turned to her. He now spoke to her, "So what brought you into this business?" She answered, "Oh this and that, you don't really want to be bored with my sob story". She by then had finished dressing and had out of curiosity, opened the dashboard. Her eyes narrowed at what she found in the dashboard. Leo turned around at the change in her voice. He was annoyed. "Why did you open the dashboard?" She gave him a sly look and asked, "Did you rob a bank or what?"

Her smile vanished when she saw Leo's face. She suddenly realized that she was looking at one of the bank robbers. She had heard about them in the news this morning. Leo said with pursed lips, "That is none of your business. Take the money I give you and get out of here." Clara laughed a silky laugh and said dramatically. "I will go away darling; only if you give me half of what you have in there." Leo smiled a tight smile, "Is that so? Okay, we have been here for a good while. Let's move and we can split the money somewhere else." She smiled, "Okay darling, let's be partners and get out of the country."   He walked over to the driver's seat, sat down and closed the door. His beer bottle was lying on the floor. He looked at Clara who was busy admiring herself while applying her lipstick. She had a mirror in the other hand. He drove the car and reached the exit to the highway. He asked her to get down so that he can get the money from the dashboard.

She got down and lit up a cigarette. She leaned on the car and pulled deeply. Leo looked at her while acting as if he was trying to get the money out. “This is the right time," he thought while he looked at her. It irritated him to see that, she was standing so smug, confident in the knowledge that she had found her golden goose. “She is in for a surprise," he said to himself with anger. He reached over and lifted up the beer bottle by its neck. He held it tight, then straightened up; both himself and his hands. He raised the bottle silently and hit her hard on the head. The bottle smashed on her skull with a crash as she was turning to look at him.

She fell to the ground with a thud and lay there motionless. Not even a cry emanated from her throat. Her eyes kept staring at Leo. Slowly blood trickled out of her skull. He stood watching her and the blood while he lit his cigarette. By the time he had finished smoking the cigarette, there was a halo of blood around her head. He was exhilarated at the sight of the blood. Another trophy for his nemesis! He then threw the butt on the ground and turned towards his car.

He gathered all the loot, he had in the dashboard and put it back into the gym bag which was in the boot. He looked at Clara one more time in disgust and sniggered. He then closed the door of the car and walked towards the exit road.

Leo walked a good distance on the highway. He saw a truck in the far distance. “It will be good to hitch hike for some time," he said to himself. He flagged down the truck and got in when the driver stopped it. He sat beside the driver. He looked around the truck. It was a private mover’s vehicle. Just the name and the phone number. No logo, no decoration or anything else. While Luke was looking around the truck; the driver was observing Luke. “Looks like you have been walking for a good while?” he asked Luke. He answered, “Yes, I have been walking for a good while now. My car stalled, the engine indicator was blinking.” He kept quiet after that. The driver did not probe any further. He could spot a liar from a distance. 'Curiosity kills the cat' but he has a family waiting for him at home. “I cannot afford to be nosy,” he said to himself.

He has given lifts to many hitch hikers in his professional life and most of the stories he had heard were lies. He has had his fair share of adventure with many of them as well. He had learnt the hard way. He kept driving. The scene outside was dark and foreboding. There were not many vehicles on the road. Occasionally one or two overtook them and then it was quite for a good while. A motel was fast approaching in the far distance. It was a pit stop for drivers and hitch hikers. "I need some food and rest. So, I am going to stop at the motel. Is that all right?" he asked. "Yes, that is fine," Luke answered. He could sense the driver's discomfort.

The driver parked the truck at the motel parking. Leo excused himself to go to the toilet. “Thank you for the lift mate. I know you want to rest; I will hitch hike with someone else. How much do I owe you?” The driver answered hurriedly, “Not necessary. I enjoyed the company. Loneliness on the highway at night, can be always dangerous. Having someone to talk to, is very helpful.” Leo saluted him and walked to the direction of the rest room. The driver got down, locked his van and walked to the reception. He booked a room for himself. He then went upstairs to his room and ordered room service. He needed a shower badly!

Leo came back from the restroom and he sat at the bar. He ordered a bottle of beer and finger food. The juke box was belting out hip hop. Some couple were dancing on the stage. Some revellers were dancing on their own as well. After being cooped in the car and the truck for so long, Leo needed some kind of exercise. He got up to the stage and danced alongside a woman who was dancing on her own. They twirled on the floor in tune with the music.

While Leo was dancing away his lethargy, Detective Dev and his team were still at the Smith cottage. They were about to finish up for the night and go out for food. However, most plans are made to be undone. 'Man proposes, God disposes'. There is no such thing as a perfect plan. Alex gets a phone call from the control room. He turned to detective Dev and announced, "There has been a homicide at Crosspool". Veronica groaned, "Oh not now! I am so hungry!" Detective Dev looked at her pointedly and Alex looked at her in sympathy. He walked to the police car and opened the dashboard. He came back to Veronica and offered her a protein bar. "The big man does not need to know," he winked at her. Veronica smiled, "Alex, you are an angel. I take back my remark from last evening; about you being a spoil sport." Alex smiled, "Oh I know that the women kind are an infidel lot!" he replied cheekily. She chewed happily on the protein bar. The three of them drove to the roadside where the murder had taken place. They picked up cups of coffee on the way to keep them going.

****

The crime scene area was covered with police vehicles. The fire brigade, ambulance and the forensic team had all arrived promptly. The area was cordoned off.

Detective Dev, assistant detective Veronica and officer Alex got out of the car into a sea of activity. The team has not touched anything yet. They were waiting for Dev to arrive at the crime scene. Dev looked around. The victim was lying face up on the ground. Her eyes were staring at an angle. Probably she had one last look at her killer before she died. The car was parked beside her or rather she was standing beside or leaning on the car and that is when she got killed. The area on the ground surrounding her head was covered in blood. Cigarette butts of various kinds were spread on the floor. This probably, was a place of frequent rendezvous for many illicit relations.

A beer bottle was lying shattered on the ground. Dev picked some of the pieces carefully with his gloved hand. It had dried stains of blood on it. "Assault resulting in trauma and death," Dev remarked. He dropped it into a specimen bag which was held open by one of the members of the forensic team. Veronica was taking notes of everything.

There was a handbag lying beside the victim. Veronica picked up the bag with her gloved hand. She opened the bag and looked inside carefully. Dev acknowledged her way of working with a smile. "You can never be too careful," he had said to her once. "You learn the basics in the academy; but the finer detail and the skills you gain on the job are invaluable. Sometimes you learn important lessons at the cost of your own health. There can be an unsheathed needle in the bag. You could get pricked just as easily."

She inspected the inside of the bag thoroughly and then pulled out a driver's license. She shined the torch light at the License. "Clara Mourners, no 3, Crosspool, Sheffield." She read out aloud; "She is 28 years old. Who is going to mourn her now I wonder?" Alex smiled. Veronica's sense of timing was always great. She had a gift of the gab and came up with the most appropriate remarks.

Once the victim's identity was established, Dev advised Alex to post out an APB to all the police station They then rang the police station in Sheffield and spoke to them. The aim was to learn more about the victim named Clara Mourners. Dev asked

Veronica to send the car registration number to the Driver and Vehicle Licensing Agency. The forensic technician stepped forward to check the License plate and take photographic evidence. He saw that the paint in the corner of the number plate was peeling off. He used his gloved hand to see why it was separating. It was a duplicate plastic number plate and the original was hidden under the false plate. He called out to detective Dev, "Sir this is the wrong number plate. The original is hidden beneath". He read out the original number of the car. Veronica quickly wrote it down and informed the dispatch. The answer came back in a flash. It was reported as a stolen car about a week ago.

Detective Dev was now concentrating on the tire mark. It looked like the car came from the East, he followed the tire marks but after a few yards, no more marks were visible. He was perplexed. Then he looked closely and saw that the existing marks were at an angle. He turned to the opposite side of the road. "No, you are wrong," he said to himself, "the car came from the West and whoever was driving did an about turn; more likely it was the perpetrator". He focused on the road coming from the West. He could see faded marks for a distance. He looked at his assistant and said, "Veronica, take the wheel please".

Veronica looked at him curiously but obeyed immediately. She knew his style of working. Obviously, he had found something. There is an old proverb 'the smarter you get; the lesser you speak'. Dev was a living example of that. She hopped into the car and turned on the ignition. He got in beside her and asked her to drive the road to the West. He instructed her to follow the tire mark. He kept leaning out of the window to have a clear view. It was cold and Veronica began to feel the chill. They drove for a good while and the mark stopped very suddenly near a wooded area. Once he saw the tire marks are about to disappear, he asked her to stop the car. He got out as soon as she stepped on the brake. The whole area was muddy; now he could clearly see the car marks coming out of the woods from the left. "Are you all right, Dev?" asked Veronica. "Yes, I am fine" he replied and came back and sat in the car, "the tire mark goes to the left into the woods". She drove into the wooded area and turned the car to the left. The car bumped up and down on the uneven gravel path. Suddenly they heard an explosion!

They both looked at each other. She quickly killed the engine and switched off the lights. They sat in the dark for quiet sometime. Neither of them made a sound. Their ears were straining to catch any noise coming from the outside. They didn't hear anything. Everything was quiet. Even the nocturnal animals were quiet. Their rhythmic breathing was the only sound that was audible to them. Eventually an owl hooted in the distance. Dev quietly opened the car and got out with his head low. He squatted on the ground. He pulled out his gun from his holster. He looked around cautiously. He waited for a while to see if there was a reaction to him getting out of the car. He then shined his torchlight and checked the vicinity. He could not see any threat. He heard a rustling sound and felt the breeze on his face. He looked down to see the dry leaves brushing against each other in the wind. His gaze continued to inspect the ground, past the leaves.

He suddenly burst out laughing. He looked up at Veronica. She was looking at him in exasperation. Her emotion of fear lifted slowly. She got out of the car. "It is not funny, what are you laughing at?" she asked him. She then looked to where Dev was pointing and burst out laughing herself. "Oh my God, it is a puncture!" Dev laughed at her louder. She is more annoyed now, "Please don't fib detective. Tell me frankly. You were also thinking that it was some kind of a gunshot!" Dev controlled his laughter with difficulty. He answered,

“Yes I know, and you are correct. It's not funny to get a scare like that”. He looked down at the source of the puncture.

A glass piece had sliced into the rear wheel of the car. He looked closely at the glass. It looked like that of a beer bottle. The logo seemed to be the same as that of the beer bottle found near the body of Clara Mourners. Veronica picked up the glass pieces and saved it in a specimen bag. “I will call for help," suggested Veronica. “Hang on," Dev stopped her. He saw something luminescent on the ground under the leaves. He took a twig and poked around. With a smile, he picked up the object. He looked at it closely. It was a woman's underwear and he could see some dry semen on it. They both looked at each other and smiled.

Veronica remarked, "So they came here, relaxed for a while and had sex?" Dev answered, "All was very well until the sex; then, something changed." He continued, "Probably had an argument. Then, it looks like they came to some kind of agreement. Whatever was agreed upon; made them drive to the murder spot. He then killed her and escaped from there".

Veronica sighed loudly, "What might have changed?" Dev said to Veronica, "While you are getting help for the car; get the forensic team as well. Otherwise this is all just going to be speculation." Veronica went to the car and radioed for help, "Officer Veronica here, vehicle breakdown in route number 1339 near the woods. We are stranded." The dispatch officer picked up the message and answered, “Help is on the way.” Dev was now looking for more clues. Meanwhile Veronica called Alex and asked him to relay the message to the forensic team. She gave him the details of what they thought had happened in the woods.

****

Leo was still dancing away in the pub. He now felt better. The dance had loosened and relaxed his muscles. He went back to the bar and sat down on a stool. He looked around for a good while and finished his beer. He paid for the services and then got up to leave. He walked past the tables adjacent to the dance floor. He accidentally brushed into a man but walked away from there without paying attention. To an onlooker it looked Leo was deep in thought. But he was actually looking at the set of keys in his hands and smiled. He now walked out into the car park and activated the remote on the car keys a few times in different directions. Eventually, he found the matching car.

He approached the car and cautiously opened it. He got in and turned on the ignition. He was about to release the handbrake when, he heard a knock on the window. He swore under his breath. He did not know who was knocking. Leo slowly raised his head and looked outside. A woman was peeping in through the window. He rolled the glass down and looked at her enquiringly. She smiled and asked, "Can I come with you?" He nodded and opened the car door. "what is your name?" he asked her. She replied as she got in, "My friends call me Nancy". Leo quietly began to drive. "He did not need this baggage at present; but nothing can be done about it. She has probably seen him looking for the car. He should have been more careful," he chided himself. He drove quietly for some time. He smiled at Nancy; who smiled back at him. The car was devouring the road at great speed. He began to think about his friends. He wondered if they got out all right?

****

Meanwhile, Frank and a sleeping Samuel were in the front seat of the car. They were in Scotland now. They had also decided to stay back as well. The local roads had helped them to lie low and escape the clutches of the police. Soon after dispersing in the woods in Hempel Hampstead, they had purchased camping kits which helped them to stay warm in the woods during the night. Frank is behind the wheel at present. The music was playing on the radio. Charlie and Jude were asleep at the back. After a while, Samuel woke up and looked around. "Where are we now?" he asked Frank. Frank looked at him and answered, "Nearly there, mate. Ten more kilometers to the toll gate". Samuel looked at his watch, "Three more hours to get to the ferry." Frank asked him, "Are you excited?" Samuel answered, "Of course, this is my first time on the ferry". Frank asked him casually, "How long were you in jail?" Samuel smiled, "Fifteen years from the age of thirty. Missed everything that I should have had enjoyed if I was living outside. Never had the means to do anything before that either." Frank replied, "Don't worry. Now you can make up for the lost time. You know!" he said with a pause; "we are all in the same boat. Might as well enjoy life; before there is a hole in the boat." They looked at each other but said nothing. Samuel very well understood the meaning of what Frank was saying. They did not have a guaranteed life like normal people. At any time, they could be caught by the police or get killed in action. Might as well enjoy life until they can't do so anymore. Frank continued to drive quietly.

The inside of the car was peaceful. Samuel began to say something, but Jude woke up. He gave a big yawn and a stretch which woke Charlie up as well. Frank remarked, "You both slept soundly!" Charlie answered, "Can you stop the car please, I need to go?" Frank pulled the car to the side of the road. They all got out and stretched. Frank carried on, “We need to be careful here boys; this toll gate is equal to crossing a border. Just tidy everything up and make sure that it is out of sight”. Once they had relieved themselves, Samuel and Jude checked the car thoroughly and kept everything away neatly. He took out a bottle of water and washed his face. Jude looked at Frank, “There is no smell on you man, all is good. You won't be pulled up for drunken driving," he laughed. In ten minutes, the men were all ready to depart. They got into the car and closed the doors.

Samuel was driving now. They have by now reached the vicinity of the toll gate. They could see plenty of cars waiting in the queue. There was heavy police activity. He could see guns and dogs. He turned around and looked at his mates, “Hang in tight there". The car owners were being questioned. The noise of the police dogs barking madly filled the air. It was an atmosphere of confusion and chaos. Slowly they reached the barrier. The car ahead of them was about to pull out. The barrier was lifting up slowly. The police constable signaled to Samuel to stop. He kept the car on idle. The policeman looked in and asked for the identification. "Your id please?" Samuel saw that the car in the front is nearly past the barrier. He suddenly stepped on the accelerator, pulled the steering wheel to the left and shot out of the barrier. The policeman jumped back in fright. Before he had time to react, the car passed through the barrier and was driving away at great speed.

With a scraping sound of metal on metal, Samuel cleared the barrier and sped off. The police panicked and hurriedly got into the patrol cars. The chase began. Samuel dodged the police as much as he can. The policemen open fire. The occupants of the car decided to retaliate. Jude pulled out the gun from under the seat and shot hither and thither. The police responded back in kind. Charlie was also shooting at the policemen from the other side. Suddenly a bullet whistled through the window and hit Frank on the shoulder. Samuel looked at him. His face paled at the sight of blood on Frank's clothes. Frank was gritting his teeth. His face was suffused with severe pain. Samuel looked around for something and pulled out the scarf from around his neck. The car veered from left to right as Samuel tried to help Frank. He said to Frank,

“Hold on mate. The helicopter will be visible in the air soon! We have to escape before that. I will get out of the highway at the first possible exit”. Frank nodded. Charlie and Jude were relentlessly shooting at the police. Samuel pulls the car into the left lane and turned into the exit at the last minute. Another bullet shattered the glass. No one was hurt this time. Jude and Charlie while keeping their head low, unclipped their belt and knelt on the floor of the car. This gave them more space and leverage. Samuel shouted above the din, “Please withhold fire when we are entering the city. We don't need casualties.”

Samuel drove very fast around the suburbs. He was in a state of panic now. “I don't want us to be caught because of my nervousness," he thought silently to himself.

He said to Frank, "We have to change the car. I will need to pull in somewhere. Guys be ready!" Frank began to look out of the window. At one point, Frank asked him to drive into the approaching basement on his right. This basement was at a bend on the road. They could hear the police siren in the distance. Samuel pulled the car into the basement quickly. He observed the cars that were parked there as they drove along. Jude asked him to pull in beside a blue car. There was an empty space just beside it. Jude quickly got out and unlocked the blue car with his skills. The others began to transfer the luggage. "Fast guys," Frank screamed. He was in pain but checked the dashboard and the seats with his left hand. Samuel was shaking badly. Jude got in behind the wheel this time. Samuel helped Frank into the back seat of the car. He asked his mate, “Charlie will you sit in the front? I can do first aid for Frank”. Charlie quickly hopped in beside Jude who slowly drove out of the car park. All of them were on edge. Police cars were speeding past them. Once all the police cars passed by, they sat back and relaxed. Jude continued to drive. Samuel helped Frank out of his clothes and inspected the wound. It's not too bad. “It had just grazed the flesh Frank," he said to his friend. Frank sighed in relief. “No wonder there was so much bleeding and burning," he smiled through his pain.

****

Back in the headquarters, Dev became very annoyed when he heard the news of the escape. Whoever was in that car were probably connected to the bank robbery. It was his gut feeling and he always listened to it. "Why did they not block all the exit routes immediately?" He asked Alex. Dev looked at him, but Alex felt it not wise to open his mouth at the time. He knew just like Dev that modern communication systems have been installed in all the vehicles. During induction, all the staff were supposed to familiarise themselves to the protocols. And yet, they slipped up when it came to the real action. No one could blame Dev for his displeasure. He spoke to Dev as if to pacify him, "Celtic connections was on this week and the police were deployed around VIP's. That might have caused the slip". Dev banged on the table in exasperation. The phone rang and Alex answered. He turned around to Dev after he finished speaking on the telephone,

"They have found the abandoned car. It was in a basement car park in the suburb". Dev answered angrily, "Obviously they were not going to wait around. Have they checked the cctv from the basement? Get the list of cars that left the exit around that time. Put out an APB for alerts for missing cars".

****

Many people were seated around the luxurious chairs in the lounge of the cruise ship. The large liner was one thousand feet by two hundred feet. It had ten levels and each level had a special feature. Either it was the casino, the swimming pool, the bar and dance hall or the kids play area. Fibre glass protected the people from the weather and yet; allowed the holiday makers to enjoy the view and the sun. There was fun and laughter in the lounge. Men, women and children were moving around in their holiday gear.

Everyone was in a good mood. The news presenter was reading the news on the television, "Last night at around 1130, four men in a car hit the barrier at a police checkpoint and were chased around the suburbs of Glasgow with no avail. They escaped from the clutches of the police. Extra checkpoints have now been installed and the police are more vigilant. We have Detective Dev in our studio to answer the questions, that the public are asking". She turned to the detective and spoke to him, "Welcome to our studio detective. There have been a series of crimes occurring around the country lately. The public have become very anxious. May I know your opinion about them?" Detective Dev looked at the news reader and answered, "Thank you for inviting me here to the studio. What I want to say to the general public is please don't be afraid. Please report to the nearest police station, anything that seems to be unusual or out of the ordinary. These people who escaped at the check post may have been connected to the bank robbery. The smallest piece of information or the gut feeling from the public will help us nab the culprit." He now stared directly into the camera. "We will get them soon."

Frank, Jude, Samuel and Charlie who were watching the news on the television in the cruise; laughed out aloud. They could not say a lot or celebrate in public, but Charlie made a symbol of a flying bird with his hands in the air. Frank declared, "Leo is giving the detective the run for his money." Charlie said, "Its good that we did not stop after switching the cars". Jude answered, "Yes, the music festival saved us". Frank told them to stop talking about it. "Guys, now that we have made it; stop worrying and enjoy what you have earned". Charlie picked up his glass of champagne and toasted, "To the detective" They all laughed, "to our freedom Charlie" and sipped their drinks. They sat enjoying their drinks in the lounge through the afternoon; way long into the evening and enjoyed the setting sun. The booze, the millions and the casual environment all helped to made them all relaxed and very tipsy.

****

Hotel Imperial was a beautiful building with red brick exterior. It was spread over an area of two to three acres. The housekeeping staff looked at the door knob of the room on the third floor. The door sign with instructions to clean the room was hanging on the handle. She opened the door with her card and went in. She began to clean the room. “Not so bad!” she remarked to herself. She was listening to the music on her mobile. 'Say the word and there is light' was streaming through the headpiece. This room was way cleaner than many of the rooms she had cleaned in the last hour. She went into the bathroom and scrubbed the place down. She then replaced the old shampoo and gel bottles with new ones. She proceeded to dust all the windows, doors and changed the screen clothes.

The supervisor had instructed her to do a deep clean of all the rooms in this floor. Yesterday was the floor below. Tomorrow will be the floor above. She was already fed up. Deep cleaning took a lot of time and elbow grease and made her tired. This happened every fortnight. She now had to clean the bed spreads. Hoover properly under the wooden bed and the floor. She took a sip of water from the bottle that she had kept on the trolley. Cleaning was always a thirsty job!

As she sipped the water, she lifted up the bed spread which was partly hanging on the floor. Her eyes grew huge and round and the bottle slipped out of her hand and dropped. The water spilled out as if in slow motion. She screamed and ran out the door. The manager had heard the scream and was coming up to see what the problem was. She barged into him and held him tight and began to cry. He calmed her down and asked her what the problem was. She gagged, "Th—there is blood all over the bed spread!" The manager was alarmed. He brought her into the reception area and got her to sit there. He instructed the receptionist to look after her. He then called the emergency services.

The hotel was surrounded by the patrol cars and more police sirens could be heard in the distance. Alex had supervised the scene while Dev was in the studio. Veronica had gone to the pathologist's office. Both of them had now arrived in separate cars. Alex acknowledged Veronica and spoke to Dev, "The house keeping staff that was assigned to this floor was cleaning the room. While she was cleaning; she saw blood on the bedspread." Dev asked Alex, "Did anyone enter the room, after she discovered the blood on the sheet." Alex answered, "No one did." Dev said to Alex, "Good. Ask the duty manager to assemble the night staff in the reception. Where is the staff who witnessed the scene first?" Alex left the room to get the night staff. Dev looked around the room with his eagle eyes. Veronica was standing with her pen poised on the notepad. She was waiting for notes and instructions.

He went to the restroom and looked around carefully. The bathroom was neat and spotless. "Too bad that she found the blood after she cleaned everywhere else. It will be difficult to get any evidence," he thought to himself. He still had to try. He looked around. Alex came inside the bathroom. “Sir, the night staff have all assembled in the foyer.” Dev repeated his earlier question, “Where is the lady who saw the blood first?” The housekeeping staff stepped forward. Alex asked her to come into the room. She looked very anxious. Dev spoke to her kindly, “My name is Detective Dev”. She nervously nodded her head. Dev continued, “Don't be afraid. Can you tell me that when you first came into the room, what did you see?” She said that she had come in at eleven in the morning and had begun to clean from the bathroom outwards. Dev asked her, “So when you pulled the spread what did you see?” He pulled the sheet as he spoke. There was a lot of blood. For the amount of blood seen on the bed, it should have spilled to the floor, but it hadn't. He was surprised. He looked at Alex and beckoned him to come closer.

Dev asked Alex to help him and together they moved the mattress. They were shocked at what they saw. They could see that a large hole has been made into the wood that was meant to support the mattress and a woman's dead body could be seen lying inside it. Dev turned to Veronica. All of them had seen the dead body by now, "That's it. Call it in. We will wait for the forensic team to arrive. Lock down the place. No one is allowed to get out of the premises. Make the staff comfortable in the dining room." He looked at the manager, "Can you organise some sustenance for the staff? They will be here for a good while and they already look tired after the night shift." The manager humbly replied, "Of course sir, I will arrange food for everyone". He instructed some of the staff. All the employees now walked away to the lower floor. Only the manager, another young woman and the policemen remained in the room. Dev asked the manager, "Do you know who she is?" The manager answered, "She was a lady of the streets. Her name was Nancy." Dev asked, "How do you know that?" The police officers standing around them smiled. The manager felt very disturbed and vulnerable. He kept quiet for a little while and then replied, "It's not like what you are thinking detective. She is a regular visitor here. She comes to this place with many of the men. That is how, I know her."

Dev looked at him for some time, "Please continue." The manager took a deep breath and then answered, “She came around 11 pm last night. I was on duty at the desk then. There was a guy with her who was young and strong. He looked fit but innocent.” He stopped talking. Dev looked at him silently encouraging him to continue. He swallowed his spit. His mouth was getting drier and drier by the minute. For a thousandth time, he wished that he was in the lower floor along with the staff who were drinking coffee and gossiping. He would give anything to be there, instead of being here and withstanding this severe looking man's scrutiny. He licked his lips and said, “I gave her room number 303. It is my lucky number as well.”

Dev looked at him and smiled, “You said that he looked innocent; I am beginning to think that you are the one who is more innocent." The manager did not respond. Dev asked, "What happened next?" The manager answered, "When the housekeeper came out of the room screaming; I was on the bottom floor checking the status of the other rooms. It is a routine practice. When she explained what she had seen, I came to the room and checked it out. I locked the door so that no one could enter and then I called the police straight away".

Dev stared at Alex who had hung his head in shame. Then he looked up at Dev in apology. The manager had not informed him that he had gone into the room; after the cleaner had reported the blood. He should have probed further or at least guessed. That is the sign of a good detective. But he fell short of his job. "A lesson learnt!" he admonished himself. Dev again looked at the manager. The manager continued to speak, "I checked the ledger immediately to see if he had checked out. So, I checked the cctv monitor. Someone had gone out past the reception at 0630. The face was not clearly recorded. He was careful to turn away from the camera. There is no one at the desk usually around the time. The desk person assists in delivering room service, so the desk is unmanned for a little while. I went to the car park to see if the car had gone as well but, the car is still here".

An officer walked in at the time and reported, "The pathologists have checked the car completely. There is nothing except for an identification card. He showed the identification card to Dev who looked at it.

He then asked the manager, “Who was supposed to be at the reception at the time?” The manager replied, “This girl over here.” The girl stepped forward and explained. “I had finished room service by 0620. I came back to the reception and then at 0625, I nipped into the toilet. I came out after ten minutes at around 0635. I am sorry that I was not there.”

Dev reassured her, “No it's not your fault. He was probably waiting for you to leave anyway. He would have hurt you, if for any reason, you had stopped him from leaving.” Veronica smiled at Dev's kindness. He had dealt with everyone gently including Alex. Not every senior officer who is investigating the crime scene is endowed with this kind of gentle nature. The entire crowd, except for the forensic team moved down to the foyer. The manager informed Dev that food was arranged for the police officers as well. Dev thanked him for his kindness but did not follow through on that.

A security guard was standing there. Dev asked him if he was on duty. “Yes, sir," he replied. Dev questioned him further, “How come you did not see him then?” The security guard looked away. Dev looked at him, “You fell asleep!" he accused. The manager was gritting his teeth in annoyance. Not only was it demeaning to him that his employee was not doing his job properly; instead of him knowing about the security guard's sloppiness; it was the detective, who discovered it.

The officer who had shown Dev the card was on the phone. He came off the phone and reported, “The car as we know from the I. D. belonged to a person by the name, Mark Anderson. He reported his car to be stolen last night from a motel at around ten o' clock. The complaint was registered at around ten fifteen at the nearest police station.” Dev nodded his head and looked at Alex, “I want all the report by tomorrow morning. Lock the city down. No one is allowed to leave.” Alex replied, “Yes sir.”

Dev asked Alex and Veronica to follow him. They went back upstairs to the scene of the crime. He stepped into the room and stood near the bed. He tried to recreate the murder in his imagination from the limited amount of information they had. He asked Veronica to come and stand near the bed. He called Alex, “Come here Alex, you are going to act as the killer. Veronica will act as Nancy".

Veronica rolled her eyes heavenwards, "She had to act as a prostitute now. That was not funny". Dev said, "There is no sign of struggle. More than likely, he had suffused her with alcohol. As we can see, she was lying naked on the bed except for, the bow necklace. She must have beckoned him to come to the bed urging him to do his business. She may have been impatient by now. They don't like to waste their time on a single customer unless it was an agreed package. She may have seen him steal the car in the motel car park; and that is why he agreed for her to tag along.

At her impatience, he must have come closer and sat down on the bed. He then straddled her and behaved as if he was enjoying her greatly. Slowly, he must have reached the nape of her neck. Alex can you do the same please?" Alex smiled at Veronica, "This is a perfect excuse to steal a kiss from you. That too, with the blessings of my senior!" Veronica retorted back viciously, "Your superior expects you to behave". Dev was oblivious to their interaction. He was self-absorbed and immersed in his theory of the murder. He continued, "He must have continued to gaze into her eyes and slowly kiss her. He will have sealed her lips with his kiss. A long deep drawn out kiss. At the same time, his thigh must have held her body tight to the bed and his hands will have squeezed her shapely neck. As we can see the flesh under the necklace is bruised. Obviously, there will be no finger print. He was careful about that. She struggled but she couldn't get her hands out from under his thighs. So, she was not able to push him off. She thrashed her legs as much as she could but to no avail. The bruise under her ankles is testimony to that. He slowly sucked out the breath of life from her lungs. This is how he killed her". Dev snapped out of his speculation and saw Veronica and Alex on the floor.

They were looking up at him in awe. He continued, "What do you think, he used for a weapon?" Alex answered that he was probably carrying a knife". Dev asked, "What about the wood though? Does it look like the mark was made with a knife?" Alex shrugged his shoulder. Veronica asked, "What about a Swiss army knife? My brother had one". Dev answered that it was more than likely. Some of the Swiss knife's have a screwdriver. The shape of the hole in the wood on the bed will fit the size of a screw driver in the Swiss knife". He continued, "It takes twenty to thirty minutes for livor mortis to set. She will be drained of blood by then. So, while she is bleeding, he stands beside her and cleans her neck, the bow necklace and her lips with water and wipes it. This will prevent leaving his fingerprint and DNA behind. He was fully clothed while he was strangling her. So, there should be no tissue under her nails. Not that she did not scratch. He must have checked the nails, he would have found that the fibre from the cloth was embedded in her nail. He used the nail clipper again from the knife and patiently clipped her nails one by one. We know the rest of the story". He extended his hand to Veronica who was still lying on the floor. He then stretched his hands to Alex and helped them both to come up from their respective positions on the ground. Together they walked down to the foyer.

****

Leo meanwhile had taken the Eurostar to France. From there he boarded the train to Barcelona. Now he was seated in an ice cream shop in Céstelό Avenue. He liked the Mediterranean sun and the dark eyed curvy women. His thoughts flew back to Nancy. He reflected back on what had happened that night. She was fun to be with for the whole night. He was not interested in sex though! His needs were fulfilled with Clara. But his intention now was to leave a gift behind; and that is exactly what he did. He had plied her with alcohol. Men get wasted after too much liqueur; whereas women will become ferocious. He had enjoyed her strength while she was struggling to escape. She had fought back with all her might; but he had overcome her with ease. He looked at her for a long time while she was lying there dead. He then checked for her breathing and there was none. He was delighted. He slowly twisted the sharp Swiss Army knife he possessed; into her lifeless body in a few places. He stabbed her mainly at the back of the lungs, straight into the heart, the liver and the kidney. Blood gushed out of her body. The nails that were beautifully manicured dropped one by one to the bed as he was clipping them. He gathered the nails into his bag. He had not touched anywhere else. All night he had been drinking from the one glass. He kept that glass in his bag as well. He then dragged the mattress down to the floor along with her body. The wooden board on the top of the bed was visible. He used the screw driver on the Swiss knife to make holes in a few places and then punched hard on the board. The board collapsed after a few attempts. He then lifted up Nancy's lifeless body which did not weigh much for his strength. It will become heavier when rigor mortis sets in. At the moment it was fine. She was still warm and supple. He haphazardly squeezed the body in through the hole in the wood. And then he replaced the mattress and the sheet. It took him about half an hour to do this. He then tidied up the place and looked at the time on the clock. It was six fifteen! He lifted up his bags, checked around for anything that he may have overlooked.

“No; the place is absolutely clean," he smiled with satisfaction. He closed the door after him, turned the door sign to the instructions to 'clean the room' and went down the stairs. On his way down, he saw that the receptionist was pushing a breakfast trolley along the foyer and knocking on the doors. He waited for her to go into one of the rooms. Instead, she left the empty trolley in the corridor and came back to the front desk. He cursed his sense of timing. Anyway, he came to the conclusion that nothing could be done about it, so he waited patiently.

In a few minutes, the girl picked up her handbag and went into the toilet across the hall. He availed himself of this golden opportunity that presented itself and escaped from there. The security guard was sitting on his chair and was asleep. "Good," he thought to himself. That saved him from killing his fellow human being. "Senor, el helado de cono que pediste," he jolted out of his reverie when he heard the voice of the lady from the ice-cream shop. He was sweating; it sounded exactly like Nancy's voice.

****

Back in London, the forensic office was bustling with activity. The place had a clinical look to it. The shelves were all full of medical, legal and pathology books. There were samples of body parts in various jars that were preserved in the liquid, Formalin. Large microscopes dotted the giant tables and were being used by the various members of the team. They were overwhelmed with the incidences of the past few days.

The team leader, who was the state pathologist; an elderly gentleman called all the team members together. They all came and sat around the table. Each one had a mug of coffee in their hands. The senior officer, Dr. Carter looked at each one of them closely. They all looked fine and focused. He could not afford a slip of any kind from his team members. All the hard work that the law enforcement puts together; can be destroyed by the defense within seconds. All they had to do was disprove the forensic findings. Their job was a delicate one. So, he needed his team members to be alert. He cleared his throat and said, "Okay folks put everything else away and concentrate on the incidents of the last few days. Do it properly but, as fast as you can. I don't want detective Dev breathing down my neck again. Consult with me before typing up your report. Is that understood?" All replied as a group, "Yes sir!"

He eventually smiled, "Vivienne, will you take care of the motel case? Take Mike with you." Vivienne smiled and replied, "Yes sir". She then looked at Mike who also got up from the table and they both moved away to one of the cubicles. He then looked at Amanda, "Dr. Smith. Can you assess both the cadavers as quickly as possible? The lab can then take care of the tests. The hair sample for the presence of drugs and to match the DNA are being processed as we speak. We now need the gastric contents from both the bodies. Please don't forget the vaginal mucosa". Amanda nodded at him and walked away from the table with her cup of coffee. Dr. Carter continued, "Michael take over the road side case, will you? Bring Daniel and Imelda with you. You have a lot of ground to cover." The three of them walked away and then Dr. Carter looked at Mathew, "Process the cars lad and let me know what you find". "Yes, sir," Mathew replied gruffly and walked off.

The television was switched on in the background and was in mute. Dr. Carter sighed. Nowadays they get the news of their various tasks from the television rather than the detectives. The lay person who calls in the incidence; first speaks to a news reporter for their ten-seconds of fame. It contaminates the crime scene and increases their workload. Yet protocol dictates that they have to wait until the detectives call them. He sighed again, “No point in procrastination," there was a lot of work to be done. Body fluids deteriorate very quickly outside the body. He watched his team doing their work for some time and then he concentrated on the reports he had to sign and send off to the various offices.

Mathew came back in about thirty minutes with the quick set dye cast of the tire marks. He then looked at the pattern with the magnifying glasses. They did not have to look for a car because the car was just there. Sometimes a clueless innocent can park a car at the scene of the crime and that is what he had to out rule. 'It is better that, ten guilty escape than one innocent person suffer' they had the quote by William Blackstone carved in their hearts. If they did not do their work properly and an innocent got punished, then there was no point in doing this job at all. The pattern of the tire near the car matched the one at the woods. So, it was the one and the same tire mark that was linking both the scenes; the rendezvous spot and the murder spot. This meant that it was the one and the same incidence. He came and informed Dr. Carter of his assumptions. His boss asked him to prepare a conclusive report on his findings. He now had to check every inch of the cars itself and that was going to take up the whole day and more. "Oh no!" he groaned to himself.

Amanda was looking on at her assistants carving out the cadavers in a y-pattern from the shoulder to the pelvis. She then began working on one of them. Clara was the first person murdered so she began with Clara. She had already examined the torso on the outside for signs of struggle. Apart from the crack in the skull there was none. The nasal sample which was full of blood was packed in a test tube and sent to the lab in the adjoining room. She took out a syringe and withdrew the gastric contents. She injected it into the sample jar that was kept open by her assistant. “Thanks Dean," she said to him and he smiled back. She then examined the lungs and aspirated the fluid from each of the lobes and saved the sample as before. She had taken the sample of the vaginal mucosa from Clara's body before she forgot to do that. Now she had the job to thoroughly examine the internal cavity and the organs millimeter by millimeter and take the required cross sections to examine under the microscope.

Vivienne had a tough time looking for the blood stains on the clothes. She had to look at samples from different places to ensure that it was blood from the one person alone. If she found a second blood sample then, she will be able to check the database to see if it was a known perpetrator.

Michael was checking out the shoe prints, Imelda was looking at the glass pieces through the magnifying glass and Daniel had the pleasant task of analysing the semen from the underwear, "Oh hello, pray tell me; who do you belong to!" he mumbled to himself.

****

Detective Dev on the other hand in his own office; was looking at the photo of the same female lingerie and asking himself the same question. Seeing his intense concentration, Veronica smiled. She was tapping away on the lap top. There was a lot of work to do. At present she was preparing the preliminary report of the case so far. Dev was oblivious to Veronica looking at him. His thoughts were now concentrated on the photos that they had got from the cctv footage of the toll gate. There were four people caught on the camera. He did not recognize any of them. Veronica can see that he is very angry. His face was like thunder. She cleared her throat and spoke, "Dev, these two murders look like they have been committed by two different people. The only commonality is that they are both call girls. But I am very confused. I can't help myself thinking that, there is a subtle message in these murders?" Dev kept quiet.

He was deep in thought. Veronica got up to go out and get a cup of coffee. Dev called her, “Veronica come back here. Can you repeat what you just said there?” Veronica turned around but stayed at the door. “I said that the only commonality is that the two victims were call girls.” Dev pondered over her words for a few seconds. “No, you said something after that.” Veronica's face creased in thought. “Oh, I asked you if there was a message in these murders. One looks like they had an argument but what about Nancy? She does not fit the picture” Dev jumped up from his chair and went to the cupboard. Veronica looked at him curiously and then shrugged her shoulders and left. She was annoyed at him. Asking questions but never replying to even one of them. She couldn't get inside his brain! Dev meanwhile opened the cupboard. His eyes fell on the photo of himself with his childhood friend, Brenda. She was smiling broadly in the photo. They both had pinned on their chest Légion d'Honneur; the French Medal of Honor for bravery. He smiled back at the photo. Something had triggered in his memory when Veronica had suggested that there was a message in these murders and now Brenda's smile had just confirmed it for him.

****

There was a knock on the door. Dev asked the person at the door to enter. Dr. Amanda Smith from the forensic department walked in. Dev turned around and looked at her. He smiled, "Come in Amanda, any progress?" She answered, "Yes, Dr. Carter asked me to personally hand deliver these to you." Dev took the envelope from her and opened it. He moved everything else away to the far corner of the table. There were DNA reports of the various samples, fingerprint traces and the report of the semen analysis. Amanda meanwhile turned around to Veronica who was back with her coffee and waved at her. Veronica smiled, "Hello Amanda, we did not expect to see you today." Dev finished looking at the reports and turned to Amanda, "Thank you for doing this so quickly, much appreciated." Amanda playfully smiled, "You can thank Dr. Carter. For once, he was the one breathing down our necks." Dev smiled at the subtle intonation. "Sorry Amanda, you know that we practically live in the office or wherever required till the case is solved," he apologised. Amanda sighed and replied, "I know detective, but the lab tests do not understand that. The reagents need time to work. The machines need the time to interpret and process the information."

Alex who had gone to see the sketch artist, walked in to the room. "The sketches are ready sir. Mrs. Ward, I mean Jennifer needed to think quite a lot to remember their faces. I think she is still in shock." Alex saw Amanda and smiled, "Oh hello Amanda, you are looking as beautiful as ever," Amanda smiled, "thank you Alex, but before you say something to spoil it, I better go." Amanda turned to Dev and said goodbye. "See you Veronica," she said and then she left the room. Alex looked mournfully at Veronica, "Am I that obvious?" Veronica laughed, "Alex your reputation is famous, be happy!"

Dev ignored their friendly banter and looked at the sketches. He smiled but before saying anything, he brought out the photos of the people he had been just staring at; just before Amanda had walked in. One of the photos matched with the sketches. He smiled more broadly. Meanwhile Veronica got up from her chair, had also joined them at the table. Now they were all smiling. Dev remarked, "Finally! The bank robbers as we suspected earlier; were the ones who escaped in the car at the toll. This other man from the sketch as described by Mrs. Ward, was the one who travelled in a separate car. He has to be the leader of the gang and the brains behind this job." He then turned to Veronica "Can you please check the database and see if any of them match?" Veronica left the room with the sketches. He kept looking at the photos, "Where are they now, I wonder?"

Veronica came back after some time. She reported that the photos did not match the national database. Alex was checking the fingerprints and DNA analysis. Neither did they match, he reported looking glum. Dev was not fazed in the slightest. He looked at Veronica and smiled. "Okay Veronica, then maybe we should speak to our neighbors. I am sure our French colleagues will have some idea." Both Veronica and Alex looked at him in surprise. "It is simple," he answered in response to their surprise; "if you can't find them here then, there can be only two more possibilities. Either they are not known to the system or they do not belong to this country. More likely the latter, I can feel a challenging note in the case. It may be that one of the bank robbers; more likely the one who was travelling on his own; is the one who is probably behind the murders. He is smart and he looks cunning. He may be moving from county to county. He is waiting until the heat dies down. In the meantime, he was also stupid. He was leaving the trail wide open. If my instinct is correct; which usually is then; he got into a quarrel with the first girl, but there is no doubt that he killed the other one for his own satisfaction. The marks around her wrist, the legs and the body fluids on the bed were a sign of struggle but there is no known cause. There can be thousands of reasons, but money is the root cause of most evils."

Veronica smiled, "I agree. What you said just now matches the time line. She thought aloud, "Rob the bank the first night, lie low, travel the second day, lie low at night, meanwhile getting bored; pick up a call girl. End up in a quarrel; possibly she has discovered the loot and he found a way out by killing her". She turned around to look at him, "But why kill the second one? The footage from the motel was not clear. Maybe he has left the country by now." Dev answered, "I am definite that he is the one and the same and that he is not here anymore. Will you please make some phone calls? We may get some results." Veronica replied, "On it now Dev. I will try and pull a few favors", and she walked away.

Dev asked Alex to check the brand names of cigarette butts that they had found in all of the scenes. His assumption was based on the fact that one particular brand of cigarette appearing in all the scenes was more than coincidence. Alex came back in a few minutes. He reported the name of a popular brand that had appeared in all the four scenes; the ward's residence, the Smith cottage and the two murder scenes. He asked Alex to request Dr. Carter for DNA analysis from the cigarette butts. It will be a weak sample and a lot of work but, the cigarette butts were the only things that were overlooked because of the huge number. Alex agreed to call the state pathologists' office straightaway.

****

The office was very busy. The room to the director's office was open. Angel peeped in the door and breathed a sigh of relief. The boss man was not in. "Aah, he could not have gone far though, no one can escape his sharp eyes. Better get my work started." She sat down on her seat and checked her mails. "Ahem, I see you are in at last!" She turned around reverently and was about to reply when the phone rang. "Excuse me sir," she turned to pick up the phone. He knew from the ring tone that it was an international call transferred by the reception. It had to be answered. He walked away from there exasperated. "She always escaped my rant," he smiled to himself. His anger never lasted with her. She always did her job on time in fairness and paid attention to detail. All her arrests were always convicted.

Meanwhile Angel spoke into the mouth piece in a sweet but polite voice. "Hello, this is Detective Angel speaking from Police Judiciaire, Paris." She listened very carefully to the person at the other end. “Oh hello Veronica, how are you?” She listened to Veronica's query carefully. “Did you try the Portuguese or the Spaniards?” Veronica smiled on the other end. She retorted back, “I tried with my sister country first. Is that wrong?” Angel smiled. She liked the fact that the British always checked out with the French first. It was hard to make out if it was reverence or scorn. Did it matter? Politics should be between countries and their leaders. Not between the people; it should definitely not happen between upholders of the law. She spoke into the phone, “Veronica, send me the photos. I will definitely try my level best to trace them”. With that she exchanged some trivial conversation and then said goodbye. She then terminated the phone call. On this end, Veronica kept the receiver down.

She smiled and thought to herself, "Angel was a sound girl. Today she was a bit withdrawn and not her bubbly cheerful self. There is always trouble in work!" Veronica faxed the photos and the sketches to Angel. She hoped that Angel will not forget to help her out in her busy schedule. She turned to Dev and informed him of her conversation with the Paris office. She then continued to update the case report on the computer. Dev walked out of the office to make a phone call to his family.

Veronica turned around at the sound of the printer. She could see the photos of prisoners in convict uniform emerging out of the printer. She crossed her fingers. She was delighted that Angel had delivered on her promise so quickly. Veronica could see the French *'Judiciaire nationale'* emblem embossed on the papers that were printing. “Hope the search ends here," she said a quick prayer. She then shot out of her seat like a bow from an arrow and grabbed the paper hot off the printer. Detective Angel was always very thorough. She had faxed a full dossier about these men.

The four men from the CCTV footage were Samuel Johnson from a shady part of Paris. He was forty-five years old and convicted for murder. He was sentenced for fifteen years and was released only last year. He was in the driver seat at the toll gate. “So, the bank robbery would be his latest crime unless he also has committed a murder after that," Veronica commented to Alex who was standing beside her. He had heard her exclaim in joy and had come in to check. The next photo was that of Frank

Michael. He was in the passenger seat. His age according to the dossier was forty-six and he was sentenced for eleven years for a robbery at the gas station. He was released two years earlier. He was also from Paris. The third photo belonged to Jude Hampton. He was a robber, but his specialty was mainly cars. He was sentenced for nine years and released two years ago. The next person was Charlie Breed and he was thirty-two years old. He was convicted for fourteen years for assault and second-degree murder. He only got out last year.

Last was the photo of Leo Jones. Alex literally snatched the photo from Veronica's hands. He recognised the man from the sketches. He read it aloud, "Forty-two year old; robbery, what kind I wonder? He was convicted only for four years. Wait, the fingerprints and the shoe sizes match for the murders." He exclaimed, "Dev was correct. Leo was the one who was responsible for both murders. Hey! We have got our murderer! Where is Dev?" He turned around to look for Dev. "I am here." Dev replied. He was smiling.

****

The St. Pancras International station was buzzing with people and activity. Trains were arriving and departing on schedule. The seats in the lounge were all busy. The departmental store on either side were glittering with luxury goods. The arched gables on the roof let the light to filter through; making the place feel light and airy. The blue and yellow Eurostar trains were awaiting the passengers. The commuters were being screened in the departure lounge.

Veronica and Alex were sitting on two of the seats that were beside each other. Dev had taken the seat across from them. He was reading the newspaper. Alex looked up from his mobile phone. He said, "Dev, the car stolen from the basement has been seen at the pier in Glasgow". Dev answered, "So they have travelled by sea. May have boarded a ship somewhere off shore. That is why there was no alert from the harbor. Ask our people to check out the car and make some enquiries with the harbor master".

The coffee table in the middle was full of case files, coffee cups, plates, cutlery and their mobile phones. The train was in motion. Alex looked at Veronica. She was working hard. He asked her, “You were planning to go to Miami with the detective, now everything is spoilt, isn't it?” Veronica grumbled, “I am used to it now. Whenever, I try to get him away somewhere; you come with a case exactly at the same time. You thwart all my plans.” They looked at the subject of their conversation. Dev was spread out on the seat across from them. He was fast asleep. They resumed their chat.

Alex asked, “So you are saying that I am the one who makes your life difficult! Okay, I promise you, once this case is solved, we will kidnap the detective and bring him to Miami. That is a gentleman’s promise! Is that okay?” Veronica smiled indulgently and looked away. She wanted the detective on his own. She quickly changed the topic, "Alex, who is coming to pick us up?" Alex opened his mouth to answer but was distracted by a noise coming from behind the transparent partition. The people on the other side were screaming and shouting. Dev woke up on hearing the commotion. Alex cautiously moved closer to the partition and looked out. One man was standing near the partition on the other side in the next cabin. He had a fork in his hands, and he was aiming it at a woman's throat. Another man also had a fork in his hand, and he was aiming it at the public to control them. The second man commanded, "Keep quiet and all of you lie down. If you don't obey, I will kill you one by one."

The public were terrified and complied. The man pointing the fork at the lady asked her for her purse, "Hand that over to me," he indicated in the direction of the purse and squeezed the fork harder on to the woman's neck. The woman was anxious but answered firmly, "Why do you need my purse? I don't carry anything of value in it." The man laughed, "Do you think, I am that naive? We have been following you from the bank". The woman was very terrified now and beseeched them, "I won't give you this money, my son is undergoing kidney transplant tomorrow. This money is for the donor. If I don't give him the money, my son will not get the transplant and he will die!"

Dev and his team heard this interaction. He signaled to Alex and Veronica. Alex got up and stood beside the door near the luggage stand. He was well hidden there. Veronica crouched behind a chair and lay in wait. Dev now looked around the cabin for something.

He saw the cutlery on the table. He picked it up and threw it on the floor with a clang. The people who were on the other side of the compartment were quiet and heard the noise. The guy who had the fork pointed at the lady came to the door of the compartment to check. He stretched his neck beyond the partition. "Bad move," he heard a voice. Detective Dev who was now standing across from Alex pulled the robber by the right hand which was holding on to the fork. He smacked him on the neck at a nerve point. It is the pressure points fighting style or *Varmakkalai.* Detective Dev had learnt it in his childhood from a master of the art. The pressure points can be triggered to heal or to cause harm. It causes intense pain, immobilises the vocal cord and can also cause unconsciousness but never death. The person becomes inactive temporarily allowing the victim to escape or to get help. This robber on the Eurostar was equally affected and fell down unconscious on the floor.

Some time passed. When the man who had gone out to investigate did not come back to the compartment, the second robber who was waiting for his pal became cautious. He swiftly but quietly moved over to the lady and held her again as a hostage with the fork pointed to her neck. The second robber called out, “Whoever is inside that room come out; otherwise I will kill this woman." A few seconds later, Alex came out of his hiding place. Detective Dev used Alex's body as a shield and was walking behind him.

The robber saw Alex who was in plain clothes walking towards him. He asked Alex, "Where is my friend? What have you done to him?" Then he called out, "Hey Leonard, you okay?" There was no answer. He looked at Alex and threatened him, "What have you done to him? I will kill you." He was very angry and pointed his fork at Alex. He was feeling some discomfort now. He was unprepared for this unexpected turn of events. He felt very vulnerable as he also knew that he was outnumbered. Moreover, his companion was nowhere to be seen. Dev smiled to himself, "Amateurs!". He appeared from behind Alex with his fork in his hand, and stabbed the robber in his thighs. The robber fell down on the floor. He screamed and swore in pain. The woman who was held at fork point, screamed in fear thinking of all the 'what if's'. She swiftly moved away from there and blended in with the crowd. The people were silent and did not know how to react. When realization dawned; they began to applause one by one and very soon it turned into a full standing ovation.

Meanwhile Veronica who was crouched behind the seat had secured both of them with the plasticuff for the hands and the legs and was standing guard over them with a fork in both hands. One move and they will be stabbed straight in the chest. Despite the seriousness of the situation, Alex could not help laughing at the sight of a fork wielding Veronica instead of a gun. He said to Veronica, "You look like Joan of Arc". Veronica retorted, "No disrespect Alex, but she was burned at the stakes by a few men. I do not intend to end up in that manner". "Well, done, people," detective Dev acknowledged both of their efforts in bringing the perpetrators down. They then calmed the public. The criminals were secured to the chairs by another few plasticuff.

The cabin was vacated and locked by the conductor on the train. Both the criminals will be handed over to the French police in the Garu de Norde, Paris. Veronica went ahead with the conductor to the control room and informed detective Angel of the event. She in return, promised to send a convoy to the train station to collect the garbage. The passengers were very happy, appreciative and thankful to the team for risking their lives to save the woman and her son. They could not imagine the situation the young man may have found himself in if, something tragic had occurred to his mother.

****

There were a good few members from the Police Nationale, waiting at the train station. Veronica handed the two men over to her French colleagues. Detective Angel was there to welcome them. She extended her hand to Veronica, "Hello Veronica, welcome to Paris." Veronica shook her hand happily. "Thank you for taking care of all the bureaucracy. We could not have done it without your co-operation." She turned around to Dev and introduced them to each other. "Angel this is detective Dev, my senior and boss and this is officer Alex who I am working with." Alex extended his hand and smiled at Angel, "Ravi de vous rencontrer". Angel smiled at Alex's amateur attempt at French. She continued to speak in the English language, "My pleasure, Alex. We have a car waiting to bring you to your hotel. It is near my office and the reception has been alerted to your arrival. Your appointment with general Dubois is at three pm." The group moved to the exit and into the cars and headed to the hotel.

****

Detective Dev and his team are now waiting few doors away from Leo's house in an unmarked car. Pierre, who was Alex's French equivalent; was sitting in another car behind them. They had been waiting there for nearly two hours now. No one had moved from their positions neither could they detect any activity from inside the house. Alex was getting impatient now. He was drumming his fingers on the steering wheel. He stopped drumming suddenly and looked at Dev, "I am impressed with General Dubois; what do you think about him?" Dev answered, "Yes, he is sound. I am glad that he has agreed for the extradition." Veronica agreed with Dev, "I was actually worried that there may be a problem with that. But I am relieved now." Alex turned back to look at Veronica, "I know, I had the same issue; but it is great." Dev answered, "There should not have been a problem at all; there are no outstanding cases against them here. According to the rules of the EEC freedom of movement of persons; they went to the

UK and then committed crimes in the British soil. The case by rights should be dealt in the UK." Veronica said, "That is a valid point; I will definitely remember that when I am leading an investigation of my own," Alex goes "Oooh, Dev, Veronica is looking forward to spreading her wings." Dev laughed, "Well Alex, if she doesn't, then my reputation as a great teacher will be destroyed."

While they were having this conversation; a man whose face and head was covered with a hoodie, walked to the door of Leo's house and knocked. Veronica was the first one to notice this; she said, "Movement at one o clock". Dev inclined his head subtly and looked in the direction specified by Veronica. He indicated to Veronica to get out of the car. They got down quickly and stealthily approached the house from behind. He went and stood beside the wall very close to the door. Veronica remained stationed behind Dev. Meanwhile the man with the hoodie was still knocking. Alex who was instructed to stay back in the car was ready for the chase. He whispered into his microphone, “Person knocking on the door now, possibly an accomplice; no activity from the inside”.

Dev asked him to wait. Then he and Veronica ran to the man with their guns. “Freeze, freeze," they both shouted. The man was alarmed and raised both his hands in the air. Alex appeared from the car and hand cuffed him. He pulled the hoodie off the man's face. He was not one of the gang members that they were so desperately hoping to see. Dev and Veronica then broke the door and covering each other's back; entered inside. Meanwhile Alex and Pierre brought the suspect into the car and after issuing the standard warning began to question the man.

Dev and Veronica searched the entire house. They did not find anyone but there was plenty of evidence to incriminate the resident of the house. They found two bullet proof vests, a few arms and ammunitions and some drugs. They searched thoroughly and found nothing else. They informed the French police about the incidence; who promised to send someone to clean up the place soon.

Dev and Veronica got back into the car where Alex was still interrogating with the help of Pierre. He eventually came out of the car and informed Dev that the suspect was just someone, who had probably come to buy or sell drugs; otherwise he was innocent. Detective Dev told Alex to hand him over to Pierre who drove him away to the local police station. He decided to use him as a bait for the other drug cases.

Veronica was waiting outside the car while Dev was speaking to Alex. She got a phone call from London on her mobile. She accepted the call, "Hello, agent Veronica here!" From the other end, the caller responded, "Veronica, this is Jennifer Ward, manager of ECC bank. I need to speak to the detective". Veronica looked at Dev who was busy speaking to Alex. She told Jennifer that Dev was busy, and she could pass on the message. Meanwhile Dev looked up. Veronica motioned to him that the phone call was for him. He walked to her. Veronica now spoke into the phone, "Hang on a second Jennifer, he is coming". Dev took the phone from Veronica who mouthed to him that it was Jennifer on the other end. Dev answered into the phone, "Hello Jennifer, how are you?" Jennifer answered, "I am good officer, I needed to tell you something." Dev replied, "Go on please, I am listening." Jennifer answered in an anxious voice, "My colleagues from the bank, went on a cruise in the beginning of May. They travelled by Aquaxebex lines from the UK to the Faroe Island. They showed me the photos from their holiday this morning in the bank and I was shocked. One of the men who had robbed the bank was in the picture. He was sitting behind my colleague who was taking a selfie."

Dev thought for a few minutes, "Jennifer can you please mail us the photos, the exact dates of their holiday and their travel itinerary?" Jennifer answered, "Okay officer, I will do that immediately. I made my colleague to wait beside me to answer your questions if required." Dev answered, "That's great Jennifer, please send me the details. I will speak to your colleague; once I have seen the photos. Please ask him if he is willing to be contacted" He further said, "Jennifer, thank you for keeping your eyes and ears open. That is a great lead that we can follow." Jennifer was chuffed. She answered shyly, "Thank you officer. I want them to be caught so that we can be absolved. No one is blaming us, but things can always be said unintentionally."

Dev kept the phone down after reassuring Jennifer and saying his farewell. He in fairness felt sorry for Jennifer and Maria. He knew that the last remark was for the benefit of her colleague who was standing beside her rather than him. People don't have to use words to hurt, actions can do the same job and probably cause more pain.

The mail from Jennifer arrived in the in-box of Veronica's phone. They looked at it. The four men were immediately recognisable. They were having a good time. Dev and his team drove away from the vicinity of Leo's house. They were all thinking alike, "Leo was not in the house. But that was not a problem anymore! Now they knew where to look for the others.

Once they were bagged, Leo will be an easy find".

"It looks like the men were spending the money they had stolen from the bank and passing time before they plan something else. It is a surprise that the notes were not picked up in spite of the all European alert. Maybe they were able to get the money laundered quickly. There are many mafia groups who will do the laundering for a sizeable commission. Money moved into Africa very quickly through the Spanish Morocco route". Things were looking up. Even if the money is not recovered, it is not a problem. These men will be going down forever with a number of counts on their head".

****

Aquaxebec lines branch office was situated in Creteil, Paris. Detective Dev and Veronica had made an appointment with this office via phone and had given them the gist of the purpose of their visit. Detective Angel had helped them to secure the appointment and had taken care of all the red tape. The manager was waiting for them. He welcomed them into the office and made them comfortable. Dev asked the manager if everything was ready. The manger replied in the affirmative, “It's all ready. In two minutes, I will get it up and running”. The printer finished printing and the manager took out the paper from the printer. He gave the reams of printed paper to both of them. They both pored over the list and marked a few names. Dev instructed the manager, “I need the details of these people. My colleague Veronica will take care of things here. We will not burden you unnecessarily." The manager thanked Dev for his consideration. Veronica sat in front of the computer and began looking for the details of the travel itinerary of the intended targets.

After collecting all the details, Dev and Veronica left the office of Aquaxebec cruise line. Dev asked Veronica to send agent '999' to the cruise ship. Veronica picked up her phone and instructed agent 999 to get ready and commence on the cruise assignment immediately. The espionage department opened up an expense account within minutes and created a perfect identity for the agent. Veronica informed Dev that agent 999 will report once in position. One day later, Veronica got a message on her mobile, "Operation 999 stationed".

****

Samuel, Frank, Charlie and Jude were having a good time in the bar of the cruise ship. They were now traveling from Faroe Island to Norway. Once they embark in Bergen, they will stay there for a few days. The Aquaxebex line was a very hospitable company. The bar was crowded. The guests were all enjoying the free drinks which was part of the package. Today they were going to have dinner in the Cabaret hall. The dancers were performing on the stage. There was a special performance by the pop queen Madam Yagani. She had been flown in from Paris as promised by the cruise management. Everyone who knew her were excited. The people were extolling praises for her performance. After the dinner was over, the entertainment manager appeared on the stage. He spoke into the microphone, "Dear patrons, I am delighted to announce, that the very eagerly awaited Madam Yagani is waiting backstage. She is ready to perform. Please welcome her by giving her a big round of applause." Everyone began to get up from their chairs and clap loudly. Madam Yagani delicately appeared on stage and curtsied to the audience. She raised her hand to quieten the patrons. It took a while for the applause to recede.

Madam Yagani began to sing melodiously and she gyrated to the rhythm of her own voice.

♪♬♫

"Waiting for someone, I am a baby bitch
I want to be touched but not by anyone
I just want you, all eyes are on me
but my eyes are only on yo----u
come and hitch, I am a baby bitch"

Madam Yagani moved around the crowd as she sang. The people strained their neck to follow her attractive figure around the hall. She sat with a few people at a table during the refrain. She then moved to another table and tickled the chin of another man. While she was singing about her lips; she went and hugged a woman's shoulder from the back. She looked at the man across from the woman with yearning. The woman leaned into her and smiled. The man was moved by the madam's action of making his partner look attractive to him.

This woman had physical presence and charm and each person in the room felt chuffed by her attention. Everyone in that room was in love with her. She moved over to the next table and got the man up and twirled a few times with him. Samuel, Frank and Charlie looked at Jude in healthy envy. Each one of them thought that they should have been the recipient of the madam's attraction. The song eventually finished and then she sang an encore by popular demand.

♪♬♫

"I am beautiful, my love says to me.
I am beautiful to his eyes you see.
Beauty is skin deep everyone says,
How can it be so, when it is in the beholder's eye?
The eye of my beloved sees the beauty in me

I am beautiful, my love says to me.
I am beautiful to his eyes you see."

The hall echoed with loud claps. Someone handed her a glass of wine and she took a sip. The sipping of the wine looked as sexy as her body and her voice. The guests were eating out of her hands. The dancers came back on stage and began to perform. Madam Yagani circulated among her admirers and handed over autographed visiting cards to whoever asked for one.

She received some gifts from her admirers who had heard her sing before. She passed by Samuel's table and gave them a flying kiss. Charlie immediately stood up and offered her his chair "would you honour us by having a drink with us madam?" "Si signor, my pleasure," madam smiled benevolently and sat down. Charlie who had not expected this was bowled over. He pulled out a chair from the nearby table and sat himself down nearly hitting the floor. Frank handed her a glass of expensive wine. They were so much in awe that they had no clue as to how to entertain her!

A few days passed by. The cruiser was sailing in the North Sea. The men were always in the bar. They were partying all the time. Agent 999 noted that this was an excellent opportunity. She entered their cabin and left it slightly ajar. She wanted to make sure that she can hear footsteps if one of them decided to come back. Her heart was beating very fast. She could hear it pulsating in her ears. She searched the cabin thoroughly. She opened the lockers under the bunk beds and saw some bags.

She pulled them out one by one and photographed them. There was a lot of fresh and crisp currency in the bag just like the one she had seen when Charlie gave tips to one of the waitresses. She was sitting with them at their table at the time. This had prompted her to snoop around. She took photographic evidence of the contents of the bag including the money. This would be enough for questioning them on the spot. But she was helpless because they were in international waters and no country can and will take responsibility. "Moreover, it will be difficult to keep them arrested on board. It will be better to let them be unaware at present and enjoy the cruise," she decided. Agent 999 then carefully extricated herself from the cabin and went back to her own rooms. She sent the message to Veronica along with the photos and her decision. Veronica sent her a 'good job' reply. She had consulted with Dev who had seconded the agent's decision.

****

The headquarters of Police Judiciaire in Paris was a building in Saussaies. It was a four-story brick building spanned over the entire block. The conference room was full of French police officers. It was a large and airy room with plenty of windows which could be opened to the outside if required.

There was a small map of France and a larger map of the streets of Paris on one wall. The wall facing the chairs was filled with a large size white board. This board was filled with information about the five criminals, the timeline of the heist, their movements across the globe over the past few months and their bios. The men and women occupying the room were looking at this board and the information presented on it. They were chatting amongst themselves.

Alex and Veronica walked in to the room and spoke to the in charge, "Detective Dev and Detective Angel will be here shortly. They are speaking to the director to get the arrest warrant and consult about the plan of the arrest." The officer curtsied to Veronica with the famous French charm and shook Alex's hand. He then began to introduce his other colleagues to the two of them. They were looking at their notes when Angel and Dev walked in to the room.

Dev thanked the officers for being so patient, "Gentlemen and ladies, thank you very much for waiting for us. I hope you are all good?" Everyone smiled at his question. Dev answered to their smile, "Good, we have plenty of work to do." He began to provide instructions. He divided them into four groups of seven. The teams were each headed by Dev, Alex, French Detective Jack and Detective Angel. "As soon as we get the message from the cruiser, we will inform you and we can commence the action. Thank you for your co-operation and hard work in advance," Dev looked at everyone carefully then gave the command to dismiss.

****

Detective Dev, Veronica and Alex went jogging on the promenade in Deauville.

They have walked for nearly an hour. They have by now done four rounds of the nearly two kilometers promenade. They then went to a quaint little coffee shop by the seaside. This coffee shop is famous for fine baking and pastries. It was a very crowded place, but Angel had rung ahead and asked the proprietor to reserve seats for the three of them. The owner of the place owed a lot of gratitude to Angel. She had helped his business to survive the Parisian mafia and their attacks on local businesses. These criminals target the popular sea shore destinations. They use it as a base for peddling their drugs to the travellers. The proprietors running these businesses are always terrified for their finances and lives.

The aroma of coffee was everywhere. Several trays contained mouth-watering baked goods. Alex piled up two full plates of assorted pastry and brought it over to their table. The staff gave him three cups of coffee to accompany their pastry. They were tired and ate the pastry with gusto. The coffee helped them to wash down the flakes. They felt satiated.

The cruise was docking here at 3:30 pm on Monday. They were eagerly awaiting the message from agent 999. Dev looked at Veronica and asked her, "Is everything all right with you? You look very subdued." Veronica looked up at him and nodded in the negative. After a while she said, "It has been a while, since we have gone home. My sister is upset as she has been separated from her boyfriend unexpectedly. I am feeling guilty that I am not there for her." Dev looked at her in sympathy, "I know this is the down side of the job. Family always comes second." Alex leaned forward to Veronica, patted her on the shoulder and said, "Don't worry Veronica; as soon as this is over, I will come with you. We will go over. You can tell her that I am not like her boyfriend." Veronica laughed, "Oh Alex, what will any of us do without you?" Dev smiled at the two of them indulgently. He knew what was happening and felt sorry for Alex. But Veronica was too blind to see it!

****

The cruise was nearly coming to an end. Samuel, Jude, Charlie and Frank were sad. They were going to land on their home soil very soon. Usually, anyone who is returning home after a long time feels happy, but it was not the case for these four people. Most of the money had finished. The only solace was that they were going to meet Leo after so many months. That usually meant a new job and more money to enjoy life.

Agent 999 was standing on the deck enjoying the fresh air from the ocean. The people were all busy packing. A few weeks had gone by with enjoyment and fun. They were also very tanned and relaxed. The people who did not tan easily went to the tanning salon and topped up on their bronze color. They will have plenty of stories to tell their friends once they get to the shore.

Agent 999 picked up her phone and dialled a number. "Hello, we are all well here and we will reach in a few hours." She saw a few people come over to the deck and watch the sea shore on the horizon. She recognized many of them. She continues on the phone. "My friend has had an emergency! He needs some help. His sister is in the hospital, she needs two units of O Negative blood and some cash. She needs some food also. Can you send one cup coffee, one slice of honey melon, some blue grapes, some green grapes and pack everything? If not, there is a possibility that you will miss something. Okay could you please arrange all of these? Thanks". She disconnected the phone. She then looked around. Jude who was in disguise in a beard and hat was standing on the deck. She was worried that her true identity will be revealed. These men are dangerous. Over the last few days; she had seen their antics. They did not trouble anyone; but the language they used, and the topics of their conversation was lewd. She could now see him approaching her, "Oh my God, I hope my identity is still intact!" Jude came near the agent and waited reverently for permission to speak. She looked up at him, "Hello". Jude was smiling now, "Madam Yagani, it was our good fortune that you were on this cruise. The evenings were very entertaining because of your talent." Madam Yagani smiled in relief, "Si signor, merci beaucoup." Madam Yagani opened the mobile which was flashing. She said to Jude, "Excusez-moi" and turned away to answer the phone. After a few minutes, she looked back with a smile; but Jude was now nowhere to be seen. She breathed out slowly, this was a very long stint for her. "Being undercover in a cruise is arduous," her handler had always said to her. "There is no place to escape. You cannot be your own self even for a minute in a cruise. Your identity will be discovered very soon. On dry land, you have different places to hide for small amounts of time," he had cautioned her. She had seen through Jude and the gang's disguise; but her team will have no clue. She had to use coded message so as not to raise suspicion; but it will depend if Dev and his team were able to encode it.

****

Dev and Veronica were sitting in the car. Their team was waiting beside them in another few vehicles. Veronica had just received the call from 999. She had written down the list of things that the agent had asked for her friend's sister. She looked at Dev in frustration, "I thought that she was going to give us a message. But she has asked me to become a messenger girl!" Dev looked at Veronica's perplexed face and began to laugh. Veronica is in fact very sweet but can be very innocent most of the times. She had a lot to learn. In fairness, they both had learnt a lot under Dev's tutelage. Controlling his laughter with difficulty, he said to Veronica, "But she did give you the message!" She looked at him in confusion. Dev said, "It is encoded, we just have to break it. Let us try and decode the message."

He kept looking at the message for a good length of time. "what does she mean? These are all colors! Is it color of the dress or the people?" He said to Veronica, "O negative blood! Blood is red in color so it should be a red suit or shirt. What does negative portray?" Veronica said to Dev, "Negative is a mathematical term, but it is also the film in a camera". Dev smiled, "Okay let's take it as the film in a camera prior to printing. What does it stand for?" Veronica was delighted that she was of some assistance and warmed up, "Negatives are usually black". Dev answered, "Okay then so, let us assume that the code is describing the color of the dresses these people are wearing. Then think that the two units is two people wearing black and red. Because blood is red but negative is the first word. What is cash?" He wrote down the word on the paper, 'C/ash?' He said, "Ash is another color. So red, black and ash?" Dev said, "Okay Veronica, let us assume that two people are wearing black, red and / or ash colored clothes".

He continued further, "The third person is probably wearing coffee or brown colored clothes. The fourth person was probably dressed in light yellow. Blue and green grapes may be the design on the clothes. What does pack everything mean?" Veronica answered "pack is synonymous to put in a container or cover. What will equate to cover in clothing and accessory-hat? Cap? Scarf?" Dev answered, "Good, assuming that our deductions are correct; we are looking for two people in red shirt/ suit, one in brown and one in yellow with designs and they are all wearing some kind of head gear or the colors of the shirt are mono chrome and the head gears are black in color." Veronica thought for a little more time, "What about a beard?" Dev smiled, "That too Veronica. Good thinking"

Dev spoke in to his microphone, "Take your positions and wait for instructions".

They can now see the cruise dock in the harbor. Dev spoke again into the microphone, "Stay alert and await instructions". Veronica was also focusing on the alighting passengers and zoomed in on them with her binoculars. "Dev, will you focus on the black suit with the red hat please? Does he look like Samuel to you?" Dev focused on the person pointed out by Veronica. He spoke into the microphone, "Alex, can you please follow Samuel who is in Black suit and red hat and his face is covered with his beard." Alex answered, "Okay Dev, will see you soon," he instructed his team to follow him. Dev continued to focus on the passengers. Jude was now visible on the visual. He spoke into the microphone again, "Angel, Jude is out in an ash colored suit and black hat. Can you please take over?" Angel answered, "Okay Dev, see you and out."

Dev looked at Veronica and laughed. "so that is the secret of the O-Negative blood and cash!" Veronica was smiling, "Agent 999 needs to work on her code. Looks like Frank is coming out of his hole." Dev spoke into the mouth piece, "Jack, the guy with the blue hat and brown suit is all yours." Jack answered in the affirmative and followed Frank. Charlie was the last one to make an appearance. Dev and Veronica have the pleasure of following Charlie. Veronica drove while Dev kept a careful eye on his prey.

Charlie, when he reached outside the port got into a waiting taxi. Veronica, who had been following the bearded and disguised

Charlie; was now on the exit lane on A12 heading in to Versailles. They have now been driving for at least two hours. It seemed longer because of the time of the day. It was six in the evening. The home going traffic was still alive and very active. It was difficult to keep up with the taxi driver. Veronica was frustrated. She was getting tired now. The siren would be a giveaway and will alert the culprits. Dev had his eyes on the taxi. He can see that Charlie has instructed the driver to go around the city before reaching the final destination. He smiled to himself, "We are behind you; does not matter where you go." Veronica was trying her level best to keep up and was maintaining a safe distance. Driving around an unfamiliar city was not the easiest task. They were now driving along the Seine River and have crossed over to the

Molineaux. Veronica was hot on the wheels of the taxi. The taxi entered Clive's bar and pub.

****

Veronica slowed the car and halted outside the pub. They kept watching till Charlie paid the taxi driver and went inside. Veronica now drove into the car park and parked. Within a minute, their team joined them. They do not get out of the car. They were awaiting detective Dev's instructions.

He spoke into the microphone, "All teams report". Angel was the first one to answer, "In the South east entrance of Clive's pub." Jack answered, "Frank is approaching the pub from the North Entrance." "Alex what about you?" asks Dev. Alex's voice comes through the line, "I am shadowing Samuel.

We are approaching Clive's pub. Will be there in five minutes. Over and out." Dev answered, "It looks like they are all meeting here! Stay in your cars near the entrances on your side. Let's hope that Leo joins them soon." He looked at Veronica, "It is your turn now. Be careful and remember to await instructions. Is that understood Veronica?" She took a deep breath, nodded and got out of the car. She closed the door of the car after her. Dev spoke into the microphone, "Veronica is going in. Team alpha you are up next." A few men and women get out of an unmarked car and entered the pub with laughter and merriment. They were all dressed in casual attire. The door of the pub opened into a dark atrium which had a lot of seating areas, alcoves and love seats. There was a stage at the end of the hall. A few people were gyrating to the sound of music which was very loud. People were finding it hard to hear each other. But the environment was very jovial and contagious. Dev was still sitting in the car outside. "Veronica are you ready now?" "Yes, I am" she replied. Dev could hear her wheeze in the background. She was very anxious and panicking. This was her first sting operation. He wanted to reassure her but in a male dominated profession, even a small chink in the armor if detected, will be exploited. He cannot do that to her. She was a sweet girl. She needed to be exposed to all of this. Then only could she progress in her career. Dev continued. "Okay, wait until team beta takes over. Then you can proceed." Veronica could hear the reassurance in his voice. She felt much better. She will have back up. She was not on her own. She could hear Dev instruct the team. "Team beta, proceed and good luck." A few men got out of another car and went into the bar in ones and twos. They did not speak to each other but went and found seats that were spread around here and there. Their colleagues from team Alpha were seated around a table and making a lot of noise. The officer positioned at the bar was serving them spiritless cocktail of orange juice. They were not allowed to drink alcohol. A sting operation in a bar and no alcohol! They liked the way Dev handled the operation except for this small detail. Not nice; but the job will get done and then they can go out and celebrate their victory. The team leader spoke into the microphone, "Team Beta is positioned and waiting to aid the damsel in distress."

Veronica heard this and smiled. She came out of the staff room. She was dressed as a cocktail waitress and was looking very sexy. She had taken care with her attire. They wore tight fitting clothes that roused curiosity but did not look indecent. People looked twice at her as she went around with a tray and collected the empty glasses. She then began the tour of the private rooms. She took her time doing the rounds of all the rooms and checked out the layout. It was a tight space and it will be difficult to extricate herself if she got caught in a cross fire. The adrenaline in her system has reached its peak and she was ready to fight. “The perks of being an assistant detective in a tactical combat unit; you have to do the unpleasant bits," she said to herself. She approached the next cubicle and found the four men spread out on comfortable couches. She knocked on the side board and entered. She asked Samuel who was seated nearest to her. "May, I take your order sir?" Samuel looked at her lecherously and asked her, "Do you have anything special for me?" His cronies found it funny and laughed heartily. Veronica bent over towards Samuel and revealed her cleavage. All eyes were on the pair of pink mounds that teased their sexuality. Veronica meanwhile gazed into Samuel's eyes and answered, "Whatever pleases the patron; we have been instructed to provide. I can also give you a special treatment if you care to visit me in my home." She looks at him and winked. The others were making fun and jeering at the exchange with the chorus of oohs and aahs. Frank wanted a little piece of this beautiful dame's attention. "Come here miss, I will place an order."

Veronica straightened and looked at Frank. She walked over to him in a sultry manner. She kept the tray on the table and enveloped her arms around his neck and gazed into his eyes. "Yes, sir! What can I do for you?" Everyone now had a beautiful view of her round tight bottoms. The fish net stocking that she was wearing revealed enough to keep the patrons interested. Frank asked for a double scotch on the rocks. "Wise choice sir" She answered and turned around to the center of the table; kept her torso bent so that the cleavage was still visible and dragged the tray to the edge with both her hands. She lifted up the tray once it reached the edge. She looked at Frank, "I will be back in a wink." She swanned away from the table and reached the staff base. "Check the acoustics," she spoke into her head phone and pulled her own head set away for a few minutes. She felt like vomiting. She placed the earpiece back in her ears. The large black van which was a few yards away from the pub was equipped with surveillance monitors. Two men were listening to every word being spoken and watching every move being made. The man spoke into the phone, "Loud and clear, proceed." Detective Dev spoke into his microphone, "Stand in position. Once Leo gets here, we will proceed." He had now seen Leo at the entrance. "Alex, Leo is near your entrance". Alex answered him in the affirmative. "I can see him detective. Waiting for your orders". Dev replied, "I will take care of them. Wait for my word". Alex said, "Okay, understood; over and out". Dev gave the order to Veronica, "Please keep them engaged Veronica and wait for my word." Veronica answered, "Yes sir." She moved into the room and kept the loaded tray on the table.

The volume in the room became louder. The men were standing up and hugging Leo one by one in their usual gesture. Samuel exclaimed, "Welcome back leader! Did you have a good time?" Leo smiled, "Thanks guys. I had a fabulous time. Did you enjoy your tour?" Veronica smiled sexily at Leo, "Would you like to order something sir?" Leo looked at her appreciatively. "May be later darling. I am thirsty, how about two bottles of beer?" Veronica smiled and replied in a sultry voice, "Right away sir." Leo called out, "Baby close the door please. You know what; bring me two bull's eyes in ten minutes? Darling make sure they are not cracked; will you?" Then he winked at her. She left the room and closed the door. She now spoke into the microphone, "Bull's eye". Dev's voice carried through, "Good performance, Veronica. You are holding out very well. Keep them busy. We need them to commit to something new and in French soil. That will increase pressure on them from both the countries" Veronica heaved a sigh of relief and mentally thanked Dev for reminding her colleagues that, this is only a performance and not her real self. It was very challenging to act as a slut and it became difficult if your male colleagues begin to think of you as one. She answered, "Thank you very much sir." Dev deciphered the undertone in her voice and was happy that she understood what he was saying.

Leo brought the room to order. "All right guys, we have to plan our new job. Keep your voices low. Even the walls have ears." He looked at each one of them. They were all quiet now and paying attention. "Did you enjoy yourself?" Frank answered, "We had a whale of a time." The men laughed at the connection to the sea and their cruise vacation. Leo spoke to them, "This job, will be take place in Iceland. Samuel interfered, "Is it a big job leader?" Charlie backed him up, "Yes if we pack a big sack, it will be great. We need something that will help us settle for a good few years. May be live in Malaysia for a while." Everyone smiled, "Great plan!" Leo took out a blue print from his pocket. It showed the sketch of a bank. "We are going to clean up this bank. It will take four weeks. We will fly out on

Wednesday night. Are you ready?" The boys all cheered, "Yay".

Dev had already entered the pub and was seated at a bar stool beside the cubicle. Alex and his team were watching the camera feed. Veronica walked in to the room with two bottles of ice-cold beer. Using this interruption as an excuse; Charlie got up and went to the toilet. Alex could see this because of the spy cam that Veronica was wearing as her earring. She bent down to keep the tray and the ear ring caught the image of the blue print. Alex saved the blue print in a document on the computer. He could now see Charlie getting up from his seat. Alex informed Dev that Charlie was going to walk out of the room. Dev answered, "Okay, over and out." Dev signaled to the crowd pretending to have a good time. One of the men walked to the restroom and proceeded to empty his bladder. Charlie walked in to the toilet. He used the urinal next to this man. Charlie was whistling to himself. He was very drunk. Dev walked in from behind and acted as if he was going to use the toilet. He clubbed the back of Charlie's neck on a pressure point with his hand. Charlie slumped to the floor unconscious. Dev now spoke calmly into the microphone, "Package secure. Get ready to move." His other colleague dragged Charlie out by the back door. The policeman posted beside the door helped his fellow officer to get Charlie into a police van. He was secured by handcuffs to the seat. He remained unconscious.

The team that was in the bar along with Dev got ready for action. Veronica brought the tray with the bull's eye eggs, pepper and salt container, salad and chilli sauce and slowly set it up on the table. Veronica looked straight at Leo, "Just to inform you that I crack cases and not bull's eyes." Leo looked at her perplexed. It looked like the waitress did not appreciate his joke. But now, he is distracted by someone appearing at the door of the cubicle. His eyes widened in shock. Dev and his team walked in. Leo and his gang looked up startled.

Dev had his gun raised in his hands. He looked at and commanded the men, "Raise your hands and lie down on the ground." They were very confused as to what was happening. They did as they were told. They moved back slowly and lay down on the floor with their hands above the head. His gaze was focused on Dev. "So detective, we meet each other again. Every minute in prison, you were the only person in my thoughts. By the way, I have to say that you looked very smart in the photo of the ceremony, when they rewarded you for stealing Linda's life. That is how, I realised that you were British." He said the last word with hatred and distaste. I kept searching you up every day and learning more about you. I wanted to see you humiliated and that is why I came to London to steal the money from the bank. But somehow you managed to get me arrested again! I tried to confuse and distract you with the two murders. I agree that you have it in you. But I will not give up. I will keep coming back for you. You destroyed my life five years ago. I will not rest until I have destroyed you. This I swear; is the promise between us.

Dev looked at him pitifully, "Leo we are all like a seed on this Earth; whether you choose to grow, or wither is in your hands. Obviously, you have chosen to wither. I will keep digging you out and throw you into the scum called the prison". "Take him away," he said to his fellow officers. The team handcuffed the men carefully and led them away. They walked them out one by one.

The people sitting in the pub were surprised that a raid was conducted without violence, without any noise or even a drop of blood. They all stood up and applauded the police team who were passing by. The fugitives were all packed into the waiting vans and the team get into their individual cars.

Veronica looked at Dev. Alex who was out of the van and had joined them had already opened his mouth by then, "What was that about?" Dev smiled, "I suppose, I have to thank Veronica". She looked at him in confusion. He looked at her and said, "Remember you asked me if there was a message in the murders?" She thought for a few seconds and said hesitantly, "Yes!" Dev answered, "That is when Leo's sketch struck me as familiar. I don't think, Mrs. Ward gave the most apt description of him to the sketch artist". He smiled and then took a big deep breath. He continued, "Before you began your training, I was then mentoring your predecessor Brenda. That was at least five years back. We had come to

France for a five-day conference. We had just solved a double murder of one Mrs. Nayagam and baby Aishwarya. I was invited as a speaker by a Charity Organisation for the delinquent teenagers; that I sponsor. During this conference, I teach them how to be street smart and to protect themselves. Brenda always joined me on these occasions. In fact, she is the one who reminded me every single day until the day we left," he reminisced about his childhood friend and junior colleague with a smile. He continued after a few minutes, "Any way; on one of the days, we had gone out to the coffee shop and were having our coffee. There was a guy sitting just ahead of us. He had a cup of coffee at his elbow; but he was not drinking it. His eyes were zeroed in on the shop that was across the corridor. Something just did not feel right about the whole tableau. I signaled to Brenda and we were watching him. After a few minutes, one of the security men from the armored car came in with a cash box. This was a time locked box. The security guard left with another box and Leo; who was the person sitting ahead of us was watching all of this. He threw a few coins on the table and walked a few meters behind the security guard. Brenda and I followed him. We were just curious to see if our hunch was correct. When the security guard reached a deserted part of the alleyway; Leo jumped him. We were ready. So, we attacked from behind and subdued him. We asked the security guard to call for help. But the unexpected happened! A gun shot was heard, and Brenda was on the floor. I can never forget that sight. Both of us looked at Brenda and the source of the shot. There was this woman who was holding the gun. I practically threw Leo at the guard and myself at the woman. We were on the floor like two tomboys. The gun was loaded, and the safety clip was pulled. It went off and killed the woman in the process. It turned out that she was Leo's sweet heart. He was beside himself with grief. Ever since he blames me for the death of his girlfriend. Before the police took him away, he promised me that he will come back for me". He heaved a sigh. Veronica and Alex were quiet for some time. Then Veronica asked him, "What happened to Brenda?" Dev laughed aloud and with affection, "She recovered in a few months. Both of us were decorated with a French medal for bravery. Now she is leading her own team".

Dev proceeded to sit in the car. Veronica moved forward to sit in the passenger seat. Alex called out to her to wait. Veronica looked at him in inquiry. Alex inserted his hands into his breast pocket and brought out an envelope. He handed it to Veronica, "I promised you that once the case is solved, I will buy you the tickets to Miami." Veronica looked up at him in surprise and joy. She was really touched, "Thank you Alex." She gave him a bear hug and went and sat in the car. Alex bent down to look at Dev who was already seated inside the car. "Detective!" he saluted. The convoy moved out of the compound one by one. Alex also got into his car and drove behind the convoy.

****

STORIES COLLECTION

We are a team of story/script writers of different genre focused on Book Publication and film production. Some are the Glimpses / Narratives of our creations. Our projects are subject to intellectual copy right. If you like our Narratives and if you are interested in film production.

Please Visit: clivestorycreations.com

CPSIA information can be obtained
at www.ICGtesting.com
Printed in the USA
LVHW041550280519
619299LV00003B/683/P